HONEY IS WHERE THE HEART IS

THE HIDDEN TRUTH

OF THE

RIDDLE OF SAMSON

From the **Narratives In The Name Thereof** series

HONEY IS WHERE THE HEART IS

THE HIDDEN TRUTH

OF THE

RIDDLE OF SAMSON

Veronica F. Patterson

House of Scribes

Copyright © 2012 by Veronica F. Patterson

All rights reserved solely by the author. The author guarantees all contents are original and do not infringe upon the legal rights of any other person or work.

No part of this book may be reproduced, stored in a retrieval system, or transmitted in any form or by any means without expressed written permission of the author-except for brief quotations for the purpose of review or comment.

Scripture references are taken from The Word of Life™ Study Bible New King James Version. Copyright © 1979, 1980, 1982 by Thomas Nelson, Inc; Complete Jewish Bible by David Stern. Copyright © 1998. Used by permission. All rights reserved.

Author photo by Twana M. James of Crochet Braids by Twana
Book cover and illustrations by Camille R. Morris
Cover photography by Robert Covington of Studio Cov, LLC

ISBN: 978-0-9987939-0-0

Published in collaboration with:

Legacy Worship Ministries/House of Scribes
Richmond, VA 23238

Printed in the United States of America

This book is sincerely dedicated...

To God, for surrounding me with people who continue to love me past the point of no return.

To Evangelist Karen Worsley, for guiding me through her program that confronted and eliminated the strongholds in my heart.
It is F.R.E.E.D.O.M.
Faith to Reveal and Eliminate the Elements that Destroy Our Mind

Introduction

From Heart to Heart

How important is the heart? It seems like a rhetorical question. We know that without a heart, blood would not circulate through our bodies. We also know without a heart, oxygen and nutrients in our blood would not get to our body parts where it is needed.

Our heart works without us having to tell it what to do. Honestly, we do not think about our heart until it has an issue. Challenges like an attack, pressure, or the occasional heart break get our attention. But those things happen to the physical organ located between our lungs behind the rib cage. What about the "heart" we cannot see?

God created us physically while giving us immaterial parts that are anatomically untouchable. In His wisdom, He understood that intimate relationship with Him is spiritual, unseen and an inward process. The heart of a person-their soul, mind and spirit-are more important to God than outside appearances. What happens on the inside affects what occurs on the outside.

After forgiveness became the balance in my life, I had to surrender my "heart" to God. I had to allow His untainted love to change my soul, mind, and spirit. Through His words and actions, He proved that His perspective of my life was better than my own.

Was it easy to let Him transform me? No. My heart challenges were more from a lack of love for myself than from other people. Since I did not know my own worth, I attacked myself, constantly reminding me of my own shortcomings. Adding more pressure, I was an imperfect person who tried to live a perfect life, hiding behind masks of pride and lack of self-esteem. And I allowed my heart to be broken, believing that unrequited love from imperfect people was worth my dignity and respect. I did not trust myself, other people, or God.

God asked me to reason together with Him. Interacting in conversations with the Lord of the Universe and through series of unexplainable life events, He proved to me that He could fix my heart. He changed my soul, mind, and spirit. My perspectives of Him, myself, my life, and other people are being transformed. Much like the caterpillar becoming a butterfly, He continues to make me into what He intended. My heart heals as I give into His love. And in my yielding to God's changes, I am pleased to present to you, Honey Is Where The Heart Is.

Pronunciations

This key is included to assist with the names of the characters. However, feel free to pronounce the names as you like. Each unique moniker is an anagram of the animal it represents. A reference page is also included at the end of the book that reveals each type of animal.

1. Anpreth *ăn-prĕth*
2. Breza *brē-zə*
3. Ch'fin *ch-fĭn*
4. Charmon *shär-mŏn*
5. Drib *drĭb*
6. Edvo *ĕd-vō*
7. Eeb *ēb*
8. Enhoy *ən-hoi*
9. Flutterby *flŭ-tər-bē*
10. Ghimmundrib *gĭ-mŭm-drĭb*
11. Hyeon *hī-ŏn*
12. Ilon *ē-lŏn*
13. Inol *ē-nōl*
14. Kippers *kĭp-pərs*
15. Larinda *lä-rĭn-də*
16. Leorio *lē-oi-rĭ-ō*
17. Letebe *lĕ-tə-bē*
18. Lino *lĭ-nō*
19. Lyf *lĭf*
20. Napreth *nā-prĕth*
21. Narchom *när-kŭm*
22. Noli *nō-lĭ*
23. Noreth *nôr-ĕth*
24. Nusdrib *nŭs-drĭb*
25. Nyohe *noi-hē*
26. Olin *ō-lĭn*
27. Onehy *ŏn-hī*
28. Onli *ŏn-lĭ*
29. Onyhe *ŏn-yā*

30. Romchan *rŏm-shän*
31. Spaw *späw*
32. Tan *tăn*
33. Tarcaprille *tä-kə-prĭl*
34. Waltsaillow *wält-sə-lōw*
35. Y'nohe *wī-nō-wē*
36. Yorcive *yôr-sĭv*

So he [Samson] said to them: "Out of the eater came something to eat, And out of the strong came something sweet." Now for three days they could not explain the riddle.

Judges 14:14 (NKJV)

Honey Is Where The Heart Is

CHAPTER ONE

His golden body lay sprawled and swollen from his meal. Satiated, he was so full that he could only lie on his back, his muscular legs dangling in the air. Not leaving a trace of what had been devoured, he had licked his great paws clean. With its edges singed with a silvery gray, the full, coarse circle of dark brown hair that encased his massive face was matted with moisture from his sweaty brow.

'Such hard work to eat,' he thought. Using his right forepaw, he patted his oversized belly. He could barely move, but he liked being constricted because of a meal. Satisfaction was what he had been seeking and he had found it.

His ears embedded in the hair about his head picked up the faintest sound of little paws. His desired to turn his head in order to hear better, but the overindulgence had taken control over his entire body.

'Whatever it is, it will pass,' he thought, so he allowed his eyelids to drape lazily over his amber eyes.

Suddenly it was upon him, pouncing on his engorged stomach. Up and down it jumped until he slowly opened one of his eyes. Boing…boing…boing…it bounced on all fours, grinning, and looking down at him with the same amber colored eyes.

"I didn't know I was to have a visitor right now," spoke Inol sleepily, as he watched a younger version of himself hopping upon his bulging belly.

"Grand One, Grand One, play with me!" Not knowing how full Inol was, Noli's trampolining tortured him. Inol allowed his body to roll to one side, but Noli, even at his young age, was already quick on his feet. He landed on all fours and began to paw at the hair crowning Inol's head, getting tangled in it.

"Not right now, Noli. I have filled myself and I am ready to take a nap." Noli continued to play in his hair and paw his face.

"Please, Grand One I got up early just to see you."

"Where is your Mepaw?"

"She went out with the others to bring back more food."

"Yes, more food. I am tired from the first outing."

"Why are you tired, Grand One? Don't the females do all the work?" Noli innocently asked. He was still enjoying getting lost in the mass of brown locks.

"Who told you that?" Inol asked, pretending to be upset. He grabbed the young one with his enormous front paws, almost losing sight of him. Peering into the amber eyes of the youngster, he pretended to frown at him. Noli was young and beautiful. He was the color of sand, not yet old enough to be darkened by the sun. And he had no hair about his head. His paws were oversized for his body, and there was hardly any hair on his tail. In fact, he barely had a tail.

"My Mepaw said that the Grand One and the other males eat while they do all the work. Is that true, Grand One?" Since Grand One's discomfort outweighed an explanation, he did not bother to argue. Again, his own offspring was speaking against the order of their kind. Such lingering rebellion: now she was beginning to plant that same seed in her son. He reminded himself to address her later. He repositioned onto his back, allowed his rear legs to relax, and placed the innocent one back on his stomach. As soon as he released him from his grip, Noli began to jump again, vaulting higher than before.

"Okay, if you are going to spend time with me today, you have to sit still," he demanded, coercing Noli to settle on his belly.

"But why?" Inol realized he had to think of something for

Honey Is Where The Heart Is

them to do that did not require much movement.

"Have I ever told you the amazing story about our family?"

"Sure you have Grand One, all the time," Noli replied. Attempting to crawl down from his seated position, Inol grabbed him before his four paws could touch earth.

"Well, this is a new story. Want to hear it?"

"A new story? Yes, I want to hear it!" and he began again to jump up and down on Inol's belly. By the third boing, Inol settled him down to get his attention.

"A long time ago…"

'How long ago was it?" Noli interrupted.

"A long time," Inol replied and began again, "a long time ago and far away from here…"

"How far away was it?"

"Not really far, but far enough."

"Okay, you can go ahead." Noli granted his elder permission to continue.

"A long time ago, and far away from here, there lived one of our kind that came before us…"

"But Grand One…"

"Noli, do you want to hear this?"

"Yes, I do."

"Okay, but you have to listen very hard to this story."

"Okay, but why?"

"This is a very special story."

"Why is this one so special?" he innocently asked.

"Well, this one is special," whispered Inol, "because in this story, the Lifegiver came to visit us."

"Really?" Noli whispered back, his amber eyes opening wide.

"Yes, Noli."

As Noli wiggled around on Inol's belly to hear the tale he was about to share, Inol realized he was extremely uncomfortable. Having the little one bouncing on his stomach had added to his discomfort. While carefully holding the young one in his clawed, padded paw, he turned over onto his left side. His belly was so extended that it landed on the ground with a slapping thud. Noli, seizing the opportunity to use it as a pillow, laid his tiny bare head on the elder's stomach. With him lying on his left side, and Noli nestled against his body, Inol began the tale of the visit from the Lifegiver.

"There was a time when our kind lived in fear of others and…"

"We were afraid?" Noli chimed in. Inol sternly spoke his name.

"Noli."

"Sorry. I forgot," and he sheepishly placed his paw over his mouth. Trying to imagine Grand One being afraid, he could barely focus and pay attention. He envisioned his elder as strong and fierce. He was enthralled with him as he told the story. His mouth was wide and his teeth huge and sharp. And when he was angry, the sound that came out was loud as the storms from the sky. Noli daydreamed off into another place imagining the Grand One defending his kind against other creatures.

"Noli, are you paying attention?"

"Yes, Grand One," he responded, the question bringing him back to reality. "As I was saying, our kind lived in constant conflict with others. Since our kind was few in number then, they outnumbered us. We had to fight for the lives of our young ones, and even had to keep watch at night. Their leader was strong like us and looked like us too except…," Inol paused.

"Except what?" Noli questioned, his curiosity taking advantage of the lull in the story.

"They were black as night, sleek and quick. They mixed with the night when there were no stars and no moon. Their eyes glowed like the color of the sun and their claws were long and sharp," Inol explained, shaking his head to make his mass of hair move, "they didn't have a crown like us and they did one thing that the Lifegiver did not like."

"What was that?" Noli asked, batting his thick lashes over innocent golden eyes.

"They ate their own young!" Inol whispered mysteriously. Noli gasped,

"They ate their own young? You mean like you eating me?" Noli swallowed the huge lump of fear in his throat.

"Yes, yes, but we respect the Lifegiver. Our kind would never eat our young ones. He taught us long ago that He loves us and the only way for our kind to thrive is to care for and protect our young ones. Lifegiver promises if we care for our young and love them, then He would love us and protect us all."

"Father, please don't fill his head with those stories." She had been listening for a few minutes. Watching the elder one being tortured by the younger one made her smile. She remembered doing the same when she was younger, pouncing on her elder's belly after he was paralyzed from fullness. Doing so caused her to believe she was the one who was in control. Her thoughts changed and the smile disappeared. Control. She no longer believed in giving up any control, especially over her life. The thought of someone else having control of her life had caused her to become distrustful and she had been that way for a while.

"Ilon," Inol asked, "how long have you been there?"

"Long enough to know that it's time for the story to end. Noli, go find Grand Mepaw. She was looking for you in the high grass."

"Okay, Mepaw." He sprung from his nestled spot and headed off to hunt for his other elder. Inol observed the young one as he reached the edge of the grass. He recognized Noli's gift to hunt as it overtook him. As if stalking prey, the young one instinctively lowered his body close to the ground, balanced on the balls of his paws, and then inched his way into the grass. Inol chuckled.

"Isn't he beautiful, Ilon? Such a sight for anyone's eyes to see."

"Yes, my offspring is beautiful. Too bad that everyone didn't get a chance to see him." As her eyes welled with tears, the overflow was contained by her luscious lashes.

Inol turned to look at his offspring. She had lain down in the clearing about a foreleg's reach from him. She was so precious to him! Her fur, tanned by the sun, had been buffed like gold. Her massive head was the perfect size for her strong frame. Her silhouette was strong, yet supple, and when she walked, she moved like waves on the water. Ilon placed her head on her paws that were in front of her. He thought he saw a tear fall.

"Ilon?"

"Yes?" She did not turn her head towards him.

"Why did you return alone?" She purposely turned her head

away from him.

"Because."

"Because why?" He waited for the answer. Her voice was so full of sorrow.

It had been more than a summer ago, but she still could not make herself forget.

"You know how the hunt makes me feel." She let her tears fall. They were not salty tears, but instead hurtful ones. Inol could tell by her whimpers that she was crying. Using all the strength he could muster, he stood to his feet. With his belly dragging the ground, he moved closer to his offspring. Laying at her side, he positioned himself beside her. He draped his forearm over her shoulders and whispered in her ear,

"Please don't cry my child. I am here for you."

She tried to hold back the tears but failed. The floodgate opened. She cried and cried. Her massive size mismatched the faint moans that she allowed to erupt from her heart. She was tired. Tired of crying. Tired of trying to understand. Tired of facing each day alone. She grudgingly believed that she had been cheated from having a perfect life and she blamed the Lifegiver.

"You know one thing that I had to learn during my long life," Inol said, trying to comfort her, "is if I trust the Lifegiver, everything else falls into place."

Immediately, Ilon's tears stopped. Her body stiffened and her demeanor changed. She was no longer his offspring that needed comfort, but an heiress with an attitude. Angrily turning her head to look into her elder's face, she snarled,

"The last thing I will EVER do again," she emphasized, "is trust the Lifegiver." She then rose to her paws and left him lying there alone.

It was late in the evening when the others returned. Finding them, Noli pounced playfully ahead of them and pretended to lead the way. He stumbled over a large stone, making them all laugh. His Grand Mepaw nudged him over and smiled at her youngling. She

Honey Is Where The Heart Is

licked him with her huge pink tongue on the spot that had hit the ground, causing him to giggle from the tickle. Sometimes his Grand Mepaw treated him like a newborn. Noli made her forget how many her years were. Using her large canines, she gently grabbed him by the scruff of his neck and carried him to the entrance of their lair. When she noticed Inol sitting upon his haunches there alone, she placed Noli on the ground.

"Go on in my young one, and I will come in a moment to put you to rest."

"But I am not ready to rest," Noli yawned back, his mouth gaping wide.

"I see you're not but go on in anyway. I won't be long," she smiled at him. "Will you purr me to sleep, Grand Mepaw?"

"Of course I will. Now be obedient and do as I ask."

His Grand Mepaw watched Noli sleepily saunter into their lair. She made sure he was inside before she turned and spoke to her mate,

"Alone again? As many of us as it is here, it seems you would always have company."

Forcing himself to, Inol feigned a smile, but he knew it was all for naught. His mate had a way of knowing what he was thinking before the thought formed in his mind. What he realized but couldn't yet quite comprehend, was that the Lifegiver had intertwined them together before either of them was born. Completing someone's sentences might be based on a thought that had been expressed before, but to know a precept in his mind as she did was power; access to it only given by the Lifegiver.

As she slowly slid to the ground beside him, Lino allowed her golden form to parallel her mate's. She moved her head gently down his foreleg and allowed her uncrowned head to rest on his huge paw. She turned her massive head to gaze up into his eyes. When he returned the gaze, she could see his sadness. Lino knew how much he loved their off-spring and that all he wanted to do was relieve her pain.

"You are still my sunray," she whispered to him. He lovingly licked her face, his tongue pausing at the bridge of her wide nose. His saliva smoothed out the ruffled hair on her brow and entangled itself in her lush lashes. The smile she shared with him ignited him to smile back.

"You are my sunray, but not hers," she reminded him.

"I know Lino, but if she only knew all that..." his mate interrupted him.

"How many times have you told her to trust the Lifegiver?" she paused, waiting for an answer. One did not come. He knew she was right. They believed in teaching by example. Sometimes their life experiences and the reactions to them were a better learning tool than what could ever be spoken.

"If you tell her to trust the Lifegiver," Lino continued, "then you have to also."

There was nothing more to say. He nudged his mate with his huge head, tickling her with the hair around his head. She rolled over on her back, allowing her huge paws to dangle in the air. His belly still full, he cautiously laid down beside her. With his mind more at ease, he waited for the sun to go down

Honey Is Where The Heart Is

CHAPTER TWO

The moon was his best friend. Sometimes, but not tonight. At its fullest, the moon loomed in the sky, high and bright. He cast a shadow on nights like this. In his mind, if he cast a shadow, he could be seen. He desired to be able to close his eyes and see through his eyelids. The problem was not his vision, but the color of his eyes. He felt the Lifegiver tricked him by making everything about him pitch dark as night except his eyes. Even though they were clear and sparkled like the sun's rays bouncing off the river, his eyes were the color of the sun. The color of the fruit that hung from trees. The color of the flowers that bloomed only at night. His stealth was uncovered by the blinking of his eyes. All he had to do was lay in the dark and wait. An unexpected snare that was easily set.

"And I am famished," Napreth whispered to himself. He raked his ever-sharp claws across his growling stomach, "what shall I have for dinner tonight?" he chuckled to himself. His cord thick whiskers twitched menacingly as he crouched deeper in the tall grass, hiding from the moon and whatever his meal would be. Then he heard a sound that caused his left ear to tremble. He slightly turned his head, allowing the faint sound to bounce around in his ear. This sound was not a familiar one like he was accustomed; either the hooves of beasts on the ground or the hide of creatures scraping against the weeds.

'What is this?' he thought. As the sound got closer, it muffled itself. Something was heading towards him. He could not decipher what it was. Then he smelled it, sweet but not savory. Then he recognized the sound of padded paws like his own. Not knowing what to expect, he held his breath and tensed his sinewy muscles. His whole body prepared to attack.

She had not been able to fall asleep. Her tossing and turning had disturbed Noli more than once, so she decided to take a night walk. Her father had warned her about going out alone many times. Lately, she just did not want to listen.

"Why bother?" she asked herself, "What good does it do to listen and do the right thing, when the right thing just brings more pain?"

The dried weeds felt relaxing against her wearied body. She knew that she had walked out of their territory, but she did not care. Anguish was her new best friend, and anger was its co-conspirator. In this moment, the last thing another creature needed to do was rub her the wrong way.

As she continued her saunter through the weeds, she realized she was not alone.

She stopped, and slowly lifted her nose in the air to her right. She inhaled deeply.

She picked up on its scent. She did not know how close it was to her, but she smelled it.

"Well, well, well. What do we have here?" Napreth growled in a low husky voice, "far from home aren't you and out in the dark all by yourself?" He allowed himself to be seen, approaching from her left. Ilon slowly turned her head, adjusting her eyes in order to see the shadow that moved towards her. She realized that he was what she had sensed.

"Not far at all," she responded, turning to face him. Nonchalantly, she sat down on her haunches, pressing down the tall weeds under her. He paused.

'Did she just sit down in my presence?' he thought. He sniffed, *'and she's not afraid either. Who is this sweet-smelling creature?'* Trying to intimidate her, he began to pace around her,

Honey Is Where The Heart Is

creating a path, "do you know who I am?" he asked.

"No, should I?" responding without fear. Even when he circled her, she did not turn her head. He sniffed again. Still, no fear. Excitement overtook him.

"Who are you?" he asked, his intimidation turning into interest.

"Why must I say? It is you who approached me. What is your name?" she asked, lying down in a more comfortable position. Napreth halted in his tracks. Now he was becoming concerned. Was this a trap? How dare she lie down like that? Was she alone? Ilon lifted her head and inhaled deeply.

"Is that fear I smell?" she chuckled, purring in between, "are you afraid of me?"

"Napreth fears no one, not even your kind," he answered sharply.

"Well then, your name is Napreth?"

"Yes, and since you have my name, what's yours?"

Ilon rose to her paws and leaned back on her haunches. She began to cleanse the dirt from her body, meticulously licking each paw pad. Although her nonchalance irritated Napreth, his intrigue got the best of him. All he could do was watch her, lean and beautiful. Even in the dark her golden hue was mesmerizing.

'What am I thinking?' Napreth shook his head to clear his thoughts.

After taking the time to clean all four of her paws, Ilon walked away from where she had been sitting. He could not believe that she just walked away from him. Before she completely disappeared into the darkness, she coyly looked back over her shoulder and purred,

"If you want to know my name, meet me here again tomorrow night." Then she turned and walked away into the night.

Honey Is Where The Heart Is

CHAPTER THREE

They believed it to be from the Lifegiver. It was so beautiful especially when the sun shined through it. Sometimes it sparkled. Sometimes it flowed. Sometimes it crystallized. Usually, something clear has no color. This substance was different. Y'nohe's tiny black and yellow striped body twitched as he admired the glory of it. Smiling, he tried to imagine himself working it as the others. Yet, for them, this was not tedious work. Their actions were blessing the Lifegiver with their purpose. He buzzed about his small community of his kind, the Eebs, making sure that his transparent wings did not disturb the others. He was always the first awake, rarely missing the chance to see the first rays of the sun reflect light throughout their community. The Eebs believed as the light bounced from chamber to chamber, it was the Lifegiver's way of saying hello to them every day.

The scent of sweet lingered in the atmosphere. It was penetrating, dousing everything in its path. Y'nohe always teased that he could not get the smell out of his wings. He had yet to smell anything more captivating from fruit or flower. An out-of-breath voice interrupted his moment of tranquility.

"Y'nohe, come quickly!" the voice pleaded through breaths.

"Nyohe, what are you doing here?" he questioned his younger sibling. In his panic, he gripped his elder brother's wing so tightly that it startled him.

"It's mother, I mean The Queen. She's sick. Come, come!"

"Where is she? What happened?"

"No time, no time!" He recognized that his younger brother was tired. Even the trim of his wings on his back had curled on their edges. He must have exhausted all his energy flying so fast to get to him. Hovering over his brother, he gently clutched him with his legs. His own wings went into overdrive, lifting himself and Nyohe from the waxy floor that they had been standing on.

"She's in The Throne Room," Nyohe finally answered over the vibrations of his brother's wings. Tingling reverberations filtered through him from his brother's legs. The sensation caused him to close his eyes and pretend that he was outside The Palace. He had yet to venture far from this place. He was not mature enough yet.

Y'nohe maneuvered himself and his passenger through the tubular halls that separated the chambers of The Palace. Each area had its specific uses. There was the place for sleeping that was cool inside when it was hot outside and warm inside when it was cold outside. There was a different room where they ate. A multitude of six-sided figures plastered the walls of this room. Each figure was filled with the liquid gold his kind created, perfected, and consumed. Everyone loved this room! A space was also set aside just for those who worked. It seemed they never stopped! But their lives were in tune with work; as if they stopped, they would lose their lives. Never stopping, always moving, creating a well-planned chaos that operated on the premise that everyone did their part.

Then there was The Throne Room. It was exquisite! The rest of The Palace was made by the workers creating a waxy substance they used to form the walls and the ceilings of the compartments. But not The Throne Room. The Throne Room was constructed from the liquid gold. The Lifegiver called it "honey." The name of the sustenance was given to them by the very first Eeb, the first one of their kind, Onehy. He passed knowledge of it down from generation to generation - how to create it, how to handle it, and how to cherish it. It was enclosed in an incredibly special container, a tiny shell

Honey Is Where The Heart Is

discovered by the Eebs when they designed their first original community. Throughout the many years, each community of Eebs kept a sample preserved from the first original batch. When this tribe of Eebs created their first batch of honey, they too preserved a sample. It was kept in a unique container that was white, smooth, and had a pointed end.

When standing in The Throne Room, it appeared to be a sphere, but it was not. It did not have four square sides either, but instead twelve six sided ones. It gave the sense of seeing many perspectives while realizing only one. Two sentinel Eebs stood ready at the door, to protect those in The Throne Room with their lives. The sentinels stood tall and strong. Their black and yellow stripes alternated evenly on their bodies, six yellow and six black. Only sentinels were born designed that way. Instead of them having their weapon on the rear tip of their bodies, they carried them at their side, ready to defend their kind at a moment's notice.

Onehy made sure that the design of The Throne Room was never for- gotten. Every Eeb learned of its structure from birth. Learning it, seeing it, and remembering it became a vital part of their existence. It was tied about their neck and written on their heart, becoming a law in their lives

Still carrying Nyohe, Y'nohe approached the entrance of The Throne Room. The sentinels could feel the vibrations of Y'nohe's wings. They recognized him by his vibrations, stepped aside from the opening to The Throne Room, and allowed him to pass. There was no door. The sentinels had been well trained to guard that entrance. Nothing has gotten beyond them to this day.

Y'nohe continued on his journey along the tubular halls, nodding at each pair of sentinels along the way. Stationed in their position two by two, Eebs believed that one could put one thousand to flight, but with two, ten thousand. The duskiness of the tube was only for a short span. The honey in The Palace was so amber, so bright, that it provided a glow. Nyohe sensed when his brother reached the entrance to The Throne Room. He opened his eyes. He delighted in being transposed from the night to the day as the duskiness of the hall exploded into the light of The Throne Room. He knew they were almost to their destination because the hall was gradually transforming into the foyer of The Throne Room. Then it happened! They moved from the realm of the hall to the dimension of The Throne Room. While their bodies adjusted in the continuum, their eyes adjusted to the light

Normally Onyhe would be seated on her throne, but not today. She was lying upon a pouf of cottony wax being attended to by her servants. Her servants were loyal, humble Eebs who lived to serve her. Their bodies were opaque, single hued and had no weapon. At the moment, they were using their pearl-colored wings to fan her, keeping her cool.

"My Queen, are you okay?" Y'nohe gently lowered the younger one to the floor, and then settled down on his knees beside his mother. Onyhe spoke, struggling to speak,

"My son," She turned on the pedestal to face him, "look at you. Such concern on your face." She smiled weakly.

"I don't understand. What is wrong with you? Your stripes appear pale." Onyhe looked down at her own form reclining on the pedestal. She had not realized her color was fading. Her golden yellow and midnight black had become ashen and gray. She looked lovingly into her son's eyes.

"It's all right. As my life fades, so will the color of my being. Here, help me sit up." He reached down behind the Queen's wings and gently positioned his arm. He wrapped his wings around the top of her body and gently sat her up. He returned to his knees beside her. He stated again,

"I don't understand. Why now?" The Queen's nodules on the top of her head vibrated. One of her service eebs appeared.

"Please bring my son a pedestal to sit on," she lovingly commanded. As Queen she did not lord over her subjects. Instead, she guided and led them with love, serving them in order that they could serve her. She understood that though she was Queen, she needed them as much as they needed her. She believed they co-labored together in order that the lives of the Eebs would perpetuate.

"My Queen, I don't need to sit. I prefer to be here, at your feet."

"Y'nohe, here, it is time for you to rise and take your position." While she spoke, the servant returned with the pedestal for him to sit on. Since she called him by his name, he realized she was serious. Sitting down beside his mother, The Queen, he struggled between being her son and her servant. He had learned so

Honey Is Where The Heart Is

much from her. How to lead, how to follow, and how to appreciate the individual lives of many.

"You knew this day would come. I've been preparing you for it since you were born. You will be the first of the Eebs, the first male Eeb to reign over this tribe. And you must find your Queen."

"My Queen? Mother, you never said anything about a Queen. You've always been my Queen." Y'nohe's wings buzzed uncontrollably.

"Brother, what's wrong?" Nyohe asked nervously, "What does Mother mean by 'Queen'? I thought SHE was Queen?" All heads turned to see the younger one standing there. He had been forgotten in the bustle of taking care of The Queen. Turning to him and draping his wing over him, Y'nohe responded,

"My brother, we didn't realize you were still standing there. We will talk more later."

Instinctively, one of the Queen's servants retrieved the younger brother from the wing of the older brother. She gently took his hand, unfurled her wings, and flew off with him. Nyohe kept looking over his shoulder until he could not see his brother or the Queen anymore. His mind could not understand yet what was going, but the vibrations in everyone's wings alerted him. Due to the paleness of the Queen, the entire palace reverberated with concern. Everyone in the Palace felt the same thing the young one felt. All knew what it meant and began to prepare.

"Here My King, help me up." He began to speak but she silenced him, "yes, I said king. You, my son, have been chosen for this. It is a new season for this tribe. But you, you must find your queen."

"I have served my Queen, you. How will I know who she is? Or where she is? What if I choose unwisely? What if…?" His mother disrupted his tirade,

"Yes, you have served me, but the Lifegiver is doing a new thing! He will create a new generation in this place, letting their gifts flow like a river in a dry desert, bringing new life and restoring the old into new. She would not be just your Queen, but she will be Queen to those who serve her. To you, she will be your heart!" The words seemed to drain her. She lay back again on the pouf that cushioned her.

"My Queen, I have watched you, and learned from you. I've played my part in the tribe. Yet, I don't know how to be a king. How can I lead those who have followed you? And how can another be my heart?"

It was not frustration that gripped him. It was fear. How could he do all that he had watched his mother, the Queen do? Her royalty amazed him. She did not command or demand authority. She was born into it. She wore it like a mantle that had been placed on her shoulders. She embraced it and understood it. She knew her purpose and fulfilled it.

Y'nohe was lost in his thoughts. Not realizing that the Queen had closed her eyes, he gently slid from his pedestal and kneeled at her side. She was getting weaker. He knew that the Lifegiver would soon send for her. Gazing into her face, he reminisced about all the times he had stood at her side when she worked. He smiled to himself, thinking,

'Yes, my mother the Queen worked.' She knew how to make a chamber, and collect the precious flower dust, and even knew how to manipulate the honey into whatever form she wanted. And all she knew; she had taught him. Leaning forward and gently kissing her forehead, he whispered,

"I am here, my Queen, right here at your side." Making himself comfortable on the floor beside her waxy cushion, he decided to spend the night there beside his mother. He wanted to be there for her when she awoke in the morning.

Honey Is Where The Heart Is

CHAPTER FOUR

"Headed out again tonight?" her mother asked. Ilon irritated, curtly answered,

"Yes."

"Do you think it's a good idea for you to be out alone?"

"I don't see what the problem is. I am not afraid. I can take care of myself."

"Oh, I am not worried about you," Lino responded, "I have a concern for whatever crosses your path." Ilon suppressed her smile. Her mother knew her well. She tried not to show her anger or frustration. No matter what mask she wore, her mother could see through it. She continued to walk towards the opening of their lair.

"Don't wait up for me. I'll be fine."

"Oh, I won't. The last time you were out, the Lifegiver sent the sun after you." Ilon had perfected ignoring the voice of others. She had gotten so good at it that even the Lifegiver's voice faded from her ears. She sauntered through the tall grass, out of their territory again. She once again found herself in the tall grass, letting it gently wipe away the dirt from her face. This time, she was first.

'I can't believe I'm doing this,' she thought to herself. In her mind she began to wonder what her father would say. She imagined his eloquent speech about what his offspring should do and how she was going against all she had been taught. For a moment she considered that her actions may affect her kind, but the thought was fleeting. The last time she had considered how others would be affected by her actions, she was the one who suffered a great loss, one from which she still needed to recover. Making herself comfortable, she settled down in the weeds, and said out loud to herself,

"Why should I care?"

"Why should you care about what?"

Ilon jumped up. He had startled her. She heard his voice before she could see him. The moon was not as bright tonight, but her keen eyes still made him out in the dark. He exited the shadows. Napreth had approached her from downwind. She had not been able to sense his presence. He was glad. He had been watching her for a moment and again, he was captivated.

'Does she realize how sweet she smells?' he wondered. "Was that fear I just saw? After last night I didn't think you could be afraid of anything."

"If you really knew me, then you'd realize I'm not afraid of anything. You just caught me off guard."

"You always have your guard up?" Napreth smirked slightly.

"Maybe. I don't seem to have any reason to let it down." Ilon sat down, unconcerned.

'Okay,' Napreth thought to himself, *'is she playing coy with me?'* "Tell me, why are you out here alone? It could be dangerous in the dark by yourself."

While they conversed, Napreth moved closer and closer to her. She realized that with each step, he was invading her space. She did not budge. Fear was not her issue. Rebellion, anger, and hurt were.

"I'm here alone because the Lifegiver decided for me that I was to be alone." Hearing her say "Lifegiver," he stopped in mid-step. She noticed the hesitation.

Honey Is Where The Heart Is

"Do you fear the Lifegiver?" she asked him teasingly. He did not respond, but he continued to move towards her. With him standing before her, he looked up at him, directly into his perfectly yellow eyes. Not one flinch. Their eyes locked. Not removing his eyes from hers, Napreth lowered himself to the ground in front of her. He faced her now. He leaned forward, causing their whiskers to touch. A spark went through both their bodies, down to their tails.

"My name," she whispered, "is Ilon."

"No, not yet," she whispered. As the reddened poppy she was hidden in opened its petals to the sun, she turned over and buried her face in its fuzzy black center.

"Just a few more moments." She grasped its soft underside and tried to pull it over her. It resisted.

"Okay, I'm up! I'm up!"

Enhoy stretched her tiny furry body, shaking the sleep from her arms and legs. She leaned over the edge of the poppy and found a droplet of dew hidden under the cusp of one of its leaves. Dew was irresistibly sweet! She stood to her feet and thanked her partner for the shelter the night before. In her journey, she had met many flowers that allowed her to stay. But the flowers were grateful. If it had not been for her leaving the precious flower dust on them, they would not have survived either.

Enhoy was different from any other Eebs. She was black and striped like the others, but her stripes were not yellow. They were unique; pure white, so white that they seemed to ebb. And she was alone. She had been alone for a while. When she was first exiled from her tribe, she was devastated. She did not understand why her Queen had sent her way. She felt alone, unloved like no one needed her, and like no one wanted her. And to make matters worse, her stripes not being golden like everyone else's just added to her troubles.

Enhoy had become a survivor. Moving from flower to flower taught her to live day by day. She was grateful. Nature filled in where a tribe was missing. She learned a lot from creation. Each flower had given her a gift. Without a tribe or a community, she was not able to make any honey, but she had been collecting flower dust from every flower she settled in. Unbeknown to her, Enhoy's body was changing with every flower dust contribution. Although she could not sense her changes, nature could.

As the sun rose higher in the morning sky, she prepared to find her next stay for the day. She believed she was led to each flower that needed her.

'Needed her,' she smiled to herself, *'I need them.'* But it felt good to be needed. She made sure to be careful to ask if she could land on them, use them for shelter, and leave her mark on them. She felt today would be a good day. She said goodbye to the poppy and went on her way, looking forward to meeting `her new partner.

CHAPTER FIVE

Inol's muscles tightened. He abruptly shifted his weight awaking Lino.

"My love, what's wrong?" Then she smelled it too.

Turning her attention to the entrance of their lair, she immediately crouched in attack mode. Inol growled deep in his throat. His body tensed causing the hair about his head to shudder. Lino bared her teeth, warning what was about to come into their presence that its life was at stake. Both were now in full protective mode.

"Why are the two of you looking at me like that?" Ilon asked. The two of them both stood there looking at her in amazement. She sauntered past them without acknowledging the obvious question on their faces. Inol was somewhat confused. Ilon was not who he expected to walk through their lair. She smelled of "them." They both demanded in unison,

"Where have you been?!"

"What?" she asked before flopping down onto the ground.

"Where have you been? You smell of "them," her father asked again, this time, sternly.

"I was out…walking." She closed her eyes. "And were you alone?" her mother asked.

"Why are you concerned if I was alone. You haven't been concerned about my being alone after all this time." Irritated, Inol's voice elevated,

"Watch your tongue. You will not disrespect your Mepaw. And again, you reek of "them." I will ask you again. Where were you?" He stepped towards his off- spring.

"I was out…with a friend. Now can I get some rest?"

"You can get all the rest you want," her father yelled, "but not in here with the scent of "them" on you. I won't have it!" He towered over her, anger filling his amber eyes. She looked up at her elder. Ilon had not seen him this angry in a while. Tonight was not a night to wrestle words with him. She lazily picked herself up, headed out the lair, and flopped down in the dusty space of their entrance. No sooner did her head hit her paw, she was asleep. Inol could only stare out of the lair at her. Lino walked up beside her mate and laid her head on his strong shoulder.

"What are we to do now?" she asked him. Almost in tears, he wearily answered,

"I honestly don't know." Standing there in silence, they watched the sun rise over the horizon. The start of the new day was plaguing them with the old situation of dealing with the rebellion of their offspring.

"You were with who last night?" his brother asked.
"Her name is Ilon."
"You told me her name already," Anpreth answered, "but she isn't what?"
"She isn't one of our kind," Napreth reiterated.
"And you were out with her all this time?"
"Yes I was."
"How could you possibly think that your actions were sensible? Do you realize what kind of trouble being with her kind could bring?"

Honey Is Where The Heart Is

Anpreth was leaner than his elder brother. His moves were quicker, and his tail was shorter. They had the same velveteen, charcoal body. The eyes were the same, but the mind behind the thought processes were not. Anpreth did as he was told. He did not like going his own way. Whatever their kind decided, that was what he did. Not Napreth. He always went against the grain. It was his nature to kick against the prick.

"But you don't understand," he explained, "I couldn't resist her. She smells sweet. Not like the sweet smell of a fresh kill, but sweet, like the aroma from a flower or a fruit. I can't explain it, but when she is around me, she is all I can smell." Remembering her scent, Napreth inhaled sharply.

"How many times have you been near this 'Ilon'?"

"Twice now. She fears nothing. And something happened between us." Anpreth's ears went straight up, and his eyes opened wide.

"What happened?" His brother had his full attention.

"Our whiskers touched." Anpreth wrinkled his brow. His tail twitched back and forth. He shifted his weight from one paw to the other.

"Wait...what?"

"I got so close to her that our whiskers touched. And a spark went through my body all the way to my tail." Anpreth chuckled. His chuckle, escalating to laughter, caused him to fell backwards from his seated position onto his back.

"Why are you laughing?"

"Why shouldn't I be? Are you sure you are my elder?" he snickered. "Just because you felt this "spark" you are willing to jeopardize our safety for someone not of your kind?" Finally able to compose himself, Anpreth challenged, him, "Where is the wisdom you claim to possess, elder one?"

"You don't understand. Even she realized in that moment that something happened between us. Besides, I like her, and she is beautiful. She seems to be as one of us wrapped in the wrong skin. And I confess, even though she is golden, she has a dark side. She is mesmerizing. I plan on seeing her again."

"Do you plan on telling our elders?"

"Of course not! I don't answer to them."

"Well then I suggest you go rub yourself against a tree. You smell of "them.""

Honey Is Where The Heart Is

CHAPTER SIX

'Such a bright morning,' she thought to herself. She struggled to open her eyes against the glare of the sun. Using her paw as a shield, her long lashes untangled and parted. The sky was vivid blue and the grass, picturesque green. She lay sprawled in a field she did not recognize. Not a tree in sight. It was fields for miles. She lifted her head and looked around.

'Where is everyone?' she thought, *'and where is the lair? What is this place?'* Ilon tried to get up but she could move. Her body felt extremely heavy.

'What is holding me?' She looked down towards her feet, seeing vines that were tightly crisscrossed over her body. She was trapped! Ilon opened her mouth to cry out for help but no sound emerged. Looking up at the sun, it seemed to shine brighter and brighter. She struggled against the vines, but she could not break free. The more she resisted, the tighter they gripped. She could barely breathe.

"*Help me, please help me!*" she screamed in her head. Nothing could escape her mouth.

Suddenly she heard a deafening roar, strong and mighty.

Then again, loud and thunderous. The powerful sound vibrated the vines. She saw him at a distance, head held high, regal and royal. Then in an instant, he was at her side. She tried to see his face, but it was hidden by the glare of the sun. He stood majestically over her, breaking the unbreakable vines that bound her. Since His presence was so overwhelming, she could only lie there. He reached down and ran his huge paw across her forehead, wiping away the perspiration.

"I can rescue you," He whispered.

"I want you to save me," she whispered back.

"What do you want to do today?" Noli was clamoring in his Mepaw's ear, "What do you want to do?" Ilon slowly opened her eyes to see her young one standing there, wiping his little paw across her forehead, and trying to wake her. She turned her head from side to side, but no one was there. Just Noli.

"Mepaw, what do you want to do today? Mepaw, you've been sleeping all day. Can you play now? Can you?" Ilon was lost in her thoughts.

'Have I been dreaming?' But it was so real. The ropes had been so tight that she could still feel them. And the sun had left its warmth on her face. She smiled. After convincing herself, she answered her own question,

"I was only dreaming.

"What's dreaming Mepaw?" Noli stared into his mother's golden eyes. She lovingly smiled at him, and explained,

"Nothing my young one, nothing. Come, let's take a walk or do you want to ride today?" Excited, he bounced around his mother's feet, waiting for her to lean down so he could climb aboard her strong back. He positioned himself at the back of her head, sprawling his legs on each side of her body. Holding tightly on each side with his front paws, he rested his head on the top of hers.

Ilon knew that he was too old for her to still carry him this way. But she did not care. He was her little one for now and she doled out all the love she could on him. She had so much extra love to give. As she thought about what she missed, her heart began to get heavy.

"Not today," she reminded to herself. She sauntered towards the tall grass, Noli hanging on for dear life. He loved his Mepaw. He only had her and the others. To him, she was the strongest, bravest,

Honey Is Where The Heart Is

and most beautiful of their kind. He always felt safe with her as she seemed never to be afraid. And now, they were off on an adventure. If only he could stay awake long enough to enjoy it.

"My King, your Queen asks for you." Y'nohe looked up from his work to see one of his mother's servants standing there. He was trying hard to stay occupied.

There was nothing else he could do but work. What was to come was to come. His mother was not alarmed by the transition about to take place. He admired her composure during times like this. She was such a queen. He was having a difficult time seeing himself as King.

"Please, let her know I am on my way."

"Yes, my King." The servant quickly left to carry his message back to the Queen. Normally in an urgent situation, Y'nohe would fly quickly to his mother. But today he needed to walk. Walking and thinking usually helped him put his thoughts in perspective. However, these particular thoughts could not be handled any ordinary way. This situation had to be planned, like writing a vision and making it plain so others could understand it.

"How can I make others understand it if I don't understand it myself?" he questioned. He found himself walking slower and slower, "maybe if I just don't show up…no, I couldn't do that. My Queen has trained me and brought me up for a time as this…what am I thinking?"

Y'nohe's inner struggles conflicted with his thoughts. As he approached the Throne Room, he heard a familiar sound. A slight buzz emerged from the room. On her comfy pallet, the Queen laid on her side with Nyohe directly in front of her, snuggled under her wings.

Y'nohe remembered those days of being small enough and young enough to cuddle beside his mother. In that position, she was all mother, no queen at all. The warmth of her fuzzy body and the constant beat of her ever-working heart lulled him to sleep every time. Nyohe had fallen prey to her spell. Approaching them quietly as not to awaken his younger brother, he kissed his mother on the forehand. He whispered to her,

"I miss those days." With a smile, she whispered back.

"I do too."

"You summoned me.

"Yes, we have a few things to talk about before the Lifegiver sends for me." Her wings, though weakened, were still able to gently vibrate, keeping Nyohe fast asleep so they could talk. It was evident by the expression on his face that Y'nohe did not want to have this conversation.

"Y'nohe, come now. Did I not teach you that the Lifegiver doesn't do anything without first revealing it to those who hear Him? Did we not know that you would be King? Did we not know that you would find your Queen? If that is true, then what is your struggle?" his mother asked him. Y'nohe's anxiety spilled over in a rush of words.

"My struggle is you. How can I possibly fulfill all you have set in place? You have guided and led us for years. Under your lead, we have defeated the Spaws, those yellow meat-eaters and have fought the giant red Noreths. Our kind has flourished, and the honey has never been sweeter. How can I ever take your place?"

"Who said you would take my place? You are not to take my place, but to create your own. Because you have faithfully served, you will rightfully lead. Not only have you served your Queen, but also your kind. Didn't the Lifegiver say that the first shall be last and the last first? You have always put me and your kind before yourself. Now it is your turn to be prospered because of it." Almost ashamed to ask her such a question, he lowered his voice,

"But aren't you afraid?"

"Afraid? No, of course not. There is a time and a place for everything. A time to live and a time to die. I've lived and now I must go so you can live. If our Lifegiver is the One of the Living, then why are you trying to hold on to the one that is dying?"

Her words were sharp and two edged, a hard truth cutting to his core. Not harsh but instead, sweet like the honey that flowed in this place. He could not deny anything she was saying. His heart was breaking and mending at the same time. He began to understand. In order for him to move forward; in order for them all to move

Honey Is Where The Heart Is

forward, she had to move forward first.
"Is there any more room on your platform?" he asked. Onyhe smiled at her son, assured that he would do well in the time to come.

CHAPTER SEVEN

Ilon anticipated the dark now. She could not wait for the moon to show itself. Standing at the edge of the tall grass, she waited for her shadow to cast itself on the ground. She heard him approaching from behind her. She knew his scent well now.

"Yes, Father. What is it?" she asked gruffly. Inol fell in line beside her, his enormous shadow over taking hers.

"Out again tonight?"

"Yes." Becoming agitated even with that one question, she knew more would follow. He sensed her irritability, but asked anyway,

"Aren't you afraid of anything?" Again, another question.

"No." She did not want to just walk away disrespectfully.

"But why in the dark? Don't you know that what is done in the dark is brought out in the open and revealed in the light?" They both stared ahead into the night. Not wanting to hurt his feelings, she did not respond as she really wanted.

"There is nothing more that can hurt me in the dark. I've been hurt enough." She stepped into the tall grass leaving her elder there standing alone. Inol watched as she moved through the grass, standing there until her movements were no longer visible, until he could not see her any longer. Then he released a roar so loud and so long that creatures for miles stopped in their tracks. Not only did Ilon hear it, she felt it. It rushed through the tall grass like a mighty wind, taking away her breath. The roar startled her, caught her off guard, even frightened her. She too froze in her tracks. For a moment, she found herself back in her dream.

"What was that?" Napreth asked her, bringing her from her reverie. "Um, I'm not sure, but no need to worry about it. We are far from there."

"I have something for you, Ilon." Napreth was totally smitten with this creature before him. He thought of her constantly. He knew being involved with her was unthinkable, but he no longer cared about the thoughts of other creatures. "I remembered you told me you don't eat meat. I found this for you." He had searched all day for this bunch of fruit. It was very juicy and some of it dribbled on his face.

Ilon smiled. It had been a while since anyone had brought her something special just for her. How strange it seemed to her kind when she began to feast on fruit and plants where they lived. Ever since she had lost her mate in a hunt, she no longer had the taste for flesh. She was grateful that Lino would take Noli out on the hunts so he could learn how to fend for himself. No matter how hard she tried, she could not make herself go

She bit into the luscious ripe fruit. Its juices spilled over onto the ground, filling the air with sweetness. Napreth inhaled the aroma of Ilon. She added to the intoxicating scent of the berries. How much more could he take?

"Napreth," Ilon spoke in between bites, "will you walk back with me tonight?" Napreth hesitated. If he said no, she would she think him to be a coward. But if he said yes, he would be walking into the territory of her kind, his enemy.

"Why do you need me to walk you back?"
"I want my elders to meet you."
"Your elders? Are you sure?"
"Yes, I'm sure. If we are going to stand together, then we must start tonight."
"You are asking me to face your kind alone?"

Honey Is Where The Heart Is

"I know. But you will be safe. You are with me and I won't let them harm you."

"If meeting your elders means I can stand with you, then yes, I will walk you back tonight."

"And thank you for my fruit. You must have gotten some of its juice on your face. Here let me clean it off for you." Before Napreth could decline, Ilon began to cleanse his face. She gingerly ran her tongue across his neck and face, removing every unseen spot on his blackened coat. When she was done, all sticky traces of the fruit were gone. He could not move. Thus far, this instance had been the most intense one for him.

'She cleaned my face,' he thought to himself, *'she cleaned my face!'* He decided in that moment that he did not want to live without her. He wondered if it was truly possible for him to have a mate not of his kind. They both would soon find out.

"Which one of you today will give me a place to rest?" Enhoy flitted from flower to flower. She was a wee bit jealous. Each one of the butter cups was the color of the sun. Their hue reminded her of the color missing from her alternating bands. She enjoyed this dancing game, like a two-step as she glided between their green leaves and sauntered around their strong stalks. As she landed on each one, her wings vibrated as if she was knocking on an unseen door. She was asking, seeking, and knocking for a place for the day. If she was needed, the flowers knew to respond to the vibration of her wings. Finally, the third one opened. She was amazed each time this happened. If anyone were to ask her to explain how the two of them knew they were right for each another, she would not have an answer. She just knew it was the right time, the right place, and the right one.

"What is that noise?" Enhoy asked. Suddenly, the buttercup collapsed over her. Its bright yellow turned to a deep red. The noise got louder and louder. She crouched low onto the cushiony center of the flower. Thankfully, the petals of the flower were dark enough to conceal her, but transparent enough to see what was out-side. Her eyes widened in horror as she watched these huge yellow and black creatures flying through the flowers, disrespecting their space. But they were not soft and fuzzy like her. Instead they looked leathery and gruff. Their stingers were designed like hers, but they were thick, long, and frightening. And there was a multitude of them! She was so afraid that she held her breath. She watched as the horde swarmed about and did not exhale until the last one passed.

Her protector's color faded back to the golden yellow. As its petals unfurled, again revealing Enhoy to the rest of the world, she noticed that all the yellow flowers in that community were also returning from red to their natural yellow color. She knew the flowers would not answer, but she asked out loud anyway.

"Who and what were they?"

"They were the Spaws," he responded.

Enhoy, jumping out of fear, quickly turned towards the response.

"I'm sorry. I didn't mean to scare you." There standing before her was the perfect mix of black and orange. The creature was perched on the leaf of a nearby flower. Its flyers were at full span. Its thin, narrow body was flanked by its oversized flyers and its antenna moved slightly in the breeze.

"Who…who are you?" she stammered, afraid and impressed at the same time by the eminence of the creature.

"My name is Narchom. I am of the Flutterby clan. You looked confused when the Spaws went through here. You've never seen them before?"

"No, I haven't. And why did all the flowers turn red like that? And she," looking downward while hovering above the one who protected her, "covered me."

"You really don't know who they are, do you? The flowers saved your life. This group has saved a lot of us, even my kind. When they hear the Spaws coming, they wrap up any creature near them in their path and they all turn red. That makes the place of refuge hidden from those who hunt us." She quivered the question.

"Hunt us?"

"Yes, hunt us. The Spaws love the meat of other creatures. They hunt anything smaller than themselves. They will even hunt larger creatures. They are known to tear creatures apart, piece by

Honey Is Where The Heart Is

piece. They can be cruel. And that is without using their weapons. Keep your wings strong. That is your way of escape given to you from the Lifegiver."

"But you didn't hide when they came through. What did you do to survive? How did you escape?"

"I can fly high in the trees. They don't like flying too far up. The secret is they lose their breath. That is my weapon against them."

"Well, my buttercup and I have already chosen one another. Do you think it will be safe to stay here for the day?"

"Oh yes, you will be fine. You are in the perfect place. The flowers here will help you if they come back," Narchom reassured her. Enhoy sighed,

"I hope they don't return."

"If they have found a victim for a meal," Narchom explained, "they will be occupied for the rest of the day."

"That's good to know. Thank you." Narchom's wings began to flutter as if in slow motion, and he hovered over the flower he had been perched on.

"It was nice to have made your acquaintance."

"Must you leave now?" Enhoy asked. She could use the company. She had been alone for quite some time. Talking to the flowers was nice, but not fulfilling. They could not respond.

"I must go now. Maybe we will meet again."

He fluttered off into the wooded area at the edge of the flower community. She watched the black and orange until he was out of her sight. She suddenly felt extremely lonely. She rested once again on the flower that saved her life. She gently tapped her feet on the padded inside of the flower bed. Instinctively, her partner released the precious flower dust, covering every inch of her body. It seemed to have a calming effect on her. She raised her wings to the sun, allowing its rays to bounce off their transparency. With her spirits lifted, she no longer felt alone. As the sun warmed her back and illuminated her white bands, she set out her plans for the next day. The Spaws would not be included in her preparations.

Honey Is Where The Heart Is

CHAPTER EIGHT

Lino smelled her first. She again had the scent of "them" on her. Lino prepared to lecture Ilon when she walked through the entrance, but she froze in mid- sentence. In walked her offspring first, but as she looked over her shoulder, she saw his eyes. They were as two small suns staring back at her. All she could see was his eyes. Lino let loose a roar that awakened the whole tribe. Napreth did not budge. He was not sure if he was glued to the ground from fright or mesmerized by Ilon's bringing him here.

"How dare you bring him here!" her elder roared again, and this time at her directly. Every muscle in her body was tense and taught. If her offspring were not standing in her way, she would have already attacked to protect her family. The clamor not only awakened the tribe, but Inol also.

"What's going on here?" he asked groggily, still partially asleep.

"Look what your offspring has done!" Inol adjusted his eyes from sleep, to awake, and then to the darkness that encased the lair. He could see the golden eyes peering from the outside in. He turned quickly to Ilon,

"What have you done? Do you know what kind of danger you have placed us in?!" His anger reverberated through their living space and out into the night. Ilon just stared at them. She had purposely positioned herself between them and him. She sat down on her rear haunches, cleared her throat with a guttural "ahem" and began to speak,

"My elders, I have seen a mate of another kind. His name is Napreth. Now therefore, I choose him for me as a mate." With his heart was breaking, her father spoke first.

"Is there not a mate among your own kind, or among another tribe as ourselves, that you can take as a mate, instead of one of these darkened creatures?"

Without batting an eye, she responded. "Accept him for me, for he pleases me well." And with the same attitude that she had calmly sat down, she arose from her haunches and walked towards the glowing pair of eyes.

Her elders were speechless. Inol instructed the others to stay inside, and he followed his offspring out into the night. Determined not to leave his side, Lino was quickly on his heels. As the royal pair emerged from the entrance, Napreth was impressed. They carried their heads high and locked their gaze on him. He could see their nose and whiskers twitching in the dark as their olfactory remembered and registered his scent. Compelled to leave, he did not. He had decided Ilon was worth this encounter.

When Ilon emerged, she purposely positioned herself beside Napreth. She wanted her elders to see that she was serious and determined that they could not change her mind. She could smell her father's anger. He was on full alert. His job was to protect his tribe and he was exceptionally good at doing that. The silence was deafening. Lino spoke first,

"What are you doing here?" she directed the question to Napreth. "My Mepaw, I just told you…"

"I wasn't speaking to you," Lino snapped at Ilon, "I was talking to HIM." She turned her focus back on Napreth.

"I'm…I'm here because of Ilon. I know our union would be a first, but I know I can be her mate."

"Your union? How can you be her mate," Lino growled, "when you are not one of us, but one of 'them'?" She spit out the words.

Honey Is Where The Heart Is

Napreth took a step towards her elders. They simultaneously crouched low in a pounce position, their ears laid back and their huge teeth bared. Napreth took another step, this time lowering his head. He lowered himself to the ground, flat on his belly, and crawled the rest of the way, stopping before them. He laid there vulnerable.

Inol's eyes stung, not from tears this time, but from the stench of this creature. For him, this scent defiled his home. But his offspring was not budging. And he knew that this battle had been lost. He looked down at this midnight colored creature trying his best to submit to their authority. He nudged Lino and motioned for her to follow him. They turned and walked back into their lair, leaving Napreth there in the dirt and Ilon sitting there in her indignation. When he knew he could not be heard by anyone else, Inol leaned over to his mate and whispered,

"We may have lost this battle, but we will win this war.

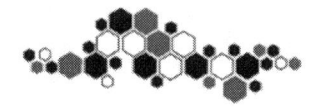

Narchom tightly closed his eyes hoping he could remember what she looked like. He needed to imprint her image in his mind. It had taken all his strength to pretend nonchalance, but now his heart was pounding wildly. As soon as he was out of her sight, he began to flutter his wings at such a high speed that he became dizzy on the way to his abode. His mate hovered at the entrance of their leafy bungalow. To him, she was the most beautiful living thing in creation. They shared the same color pattern, yet her colors were deeper. As he neared her, she witnessed the excitement permeating from his wings.

"Charmon, Charmon, I saw her, I saw her!" He was out of breath when he entered their leafy domain.

"Saw who?" Charmon questioned. Her orange and black wings were tipped with white. Her body was slim and narrow like his, but the indentation that separated her top and bottom sections were more pronounced. It was there Narchom slipped one of his legs and spun her around and around. They created a pinwheel, alternating black and orange, with a touch of white. Dizzy from their dance, Narchom finally slowed down to speak,

"It was her! It was her! The one from my visions! The scene came to life before my very eyes!"

"You saw the one that will bring change to creation? Where was she? What happened?"

"For a moment I didn't believe what I was privy to," he explained, "but when I saw the buttercup go red, covering her as if she was covered with blood, I knew it was my vision." In order to calm himself, Narchom took some deep breaths. Patting one of his antennae, Charmon encouraged,

"You should believe when the Lifegiver speaks to you. He doesn't do anything without first revealing it to those who hear Him. And besides, you know that when the Lifegiver sends out a vision, it doesn't come back to Him without filling its purpose."

With the help of her calming gesture, Narchom settled himself. In his mind, he knew that the Lifegiver operated in ways he could not always understand. But in his heart, he was overwhelmed. He had been chosen by the Lifegiver to witness what was to come. As much as he tried, he could never explain what he felt during the moments like this. Charmon's voice interrupted his thoughts.

"Tell me what you saw!"

"I saw her, the Eeb that was black and white instead of encircled in yellow. And the Spaws flew right by her. She had been protected, covered in red, just like I envisioned. Except, when I saw her in my vision covered in red, I thought it was blood and that she was in danger. But instead, she was protected by the blood, I mean, by the flower!"

"What does all this mean?" Charmon questioned excitedly.

"Creation awaits for the revelation of the Lifegiver to be revealed! It is as the Lifegiver promised. He said He would restore to us the years that creation has suffered. No longer will we be replenished by the former rain, but we shall also bask in the latter rain!" Charmon clapped her beautiful flyers together, creating a joyful noise to the Lifegiver. She repeated over and again,

"Sing unto the Lifegiver for He has triumphed gloriously. Let the one who shall bring change be protected from those who may bring harm to her."

Honey Is Where The Heart Is

'Such a bright morning,' she thought to herself as she struggled to open her eyes against the glare of the sun. Using her translucent wing as a shield, she slowly parted her eyes. The sky was vivid blue and the grass, picturesque green. She lay sprawled in the center of a flower that she did not recognize. Not another flower in sight. It was fields for miles. She lifted her head and looked around.

'Where are all the flowers?' she thought, *'and where are the trees? What is this place?'* Enhoy tried to get up but she could not move. Her tiny body felt extremely heavy.

'What is holding me?' She looked down towards her wee feet, seeing filaments of the of the flower that were tightly crisscrossed over her body. She was trapped! Enhoy opened her mouth to cry out for help but no sound came out. Looking up at the sun, it seemed to shine brighter and brighter. She struggled against the filaments, but she could not break free. The more she resisted, the tighter they gripped. She could barely breathe.

'Help me, please help me!' she screamed in her head. Nothing could escape her mouth. Suddenly she heard a deafening roar, strong and mighty. Then again, loud and thunderous. The powerful sound vibrated the filaments. Through the space between the flower petals, she saw Him at a distance head held high, regal and royal. Then in an instant, He was at her side. She tried to see His face, but it was hidden by the glare of the sun. He stood majestically over her, breaking the unbreakable filaments that bound her. Since His presence was so overwhelming, she could only lay there. Using one of the digits of His huge paw, He reached down and wiped across her tiny forehead, clearing away miniscule drops of perspiration.

"I have something for you," He whispered.

"I want whatever you have for me," she whispered back.

He opened his mouth wide and reached inside, retrieving one of his teeth. It was white, smooth, and pointed on the end. By the time He laid it upon her, it was tinier than she. She crossed her arms over it and hugged it close to her body. The harder she squeezed the softer it became. The dampness from the flower petal she was squeezing woke her up. The hairs on her arms were sticky from its nectar.

"Oh no, look what I've done!" Still embracing it, she caressed the limp petal, "I'm so sorry. I don't know what came over me."

The flower lowered another petal that gently tapped the top of her head. She could not tell if the flower did it on its own or if the soft breeze blowing over the field caused it to happen. At the moment, for her it didn't matter. She had never experienced this feeling before. It was a peace beyond any understanding.

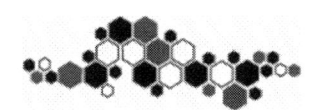

Tired, dirty, and thirsty, he had been walking for such a long time. He was so hungry that starvation had become his companion. He did not know where he was going, but he knew his paw steps were being ordered. Every morning that he awoke, the desire to move forward overcame the urge to give up. Days ago, while taking a much-needed drink of water from a muddy puddle, he wearily stared at himself. It was difficult for him to remember what he used to look like before he began this journey. The only thing he recognized was his own clear, piercing, amber eyes.

Honey Is Where The Heart Is

CHAPTER NINE

He had observed the Queen, his mother, operate in her strength his whole life. Now it was his turn to be strong. Today was the first time that Y'nohe did not want to do any work. He had crawled into a waxy chamber the night before, hoping if he fell asleep, when he woke up it would all just be a bad dream. Instead when he woke up, the first thing on his mind was the Queen. Not his mother, but the one whose place he would take. While nestling in the chamber, he had an epiphany. With all the wisdom and knowledge his mother had, he had not thought to ask her if she knew the identity of the new queen.

Feeling refreshed from his newfound idea, Y'nohe crawled out of the chamber. He stood tall, unfurled his wings, and stretched. Brushing particles off his fuzzy body, he high stepped his way toward the Throne Room. No need to fly. His spirits soared, his mind was clear, and his heart was light. Wondering if his Queen could really tell him something about his future queen, his excitement increased as he approached his destination.

She was still lying on her pouf upon the platform. The Queen had gotten so weak that walking had become an issue. Her servants fluttered about her, making a fuss amongst one another if they felt one was lacking in her care. When Y'nohe entered the Throne Room, all the servants bowed immediately. He stopped. Their actions caught him off guard because they were in the middle of their work. It caught him off guard. He almost advised them to stand, but the Queen motioned for him not to speak or reprimand them. Respecting her instruction, he continued his way across the room to his mother. Y'nohe gently pressed his lips against his mother's forehead. Still bowed in humility, the servants did not move. Now so near to his mother, she whispered,

"They will remain like that all day if you don't release them," and she let out a faint giggle. In the midst of his worries, he had forgotten his mother's sense of humor. Standing up and placing his hands behind his back, he turned towards the servants and stated,

"You have all done such good work caring for the Queen. You may go now. We will be fine alone for a while." The servants replied with a nod. They collected their items and quietly left the room. Y'nohe watched them leave. He was humbled by their humility. Turning his attention back to his mother, he asked,

"Do they ever speak?"

"Rarely. When I try to have conversation with them, they get a look of fear, as if they are not supposed to have conversation with me. Even the Lifegiver desires creation to speak with Him. Did He not say, 'let us reason together'? We are not to be fearful but in awe of Him. For years I've tried to get them to understand that. Maybe your queen will do better than me in that aspect." And she giggled again, louder this time.

"Mother, you have been 'giggling' a lot lately. Is there reason for this new aspect of your character?"

"I have been, haven't I? It's because there is a fountain, a wellspring within me. Because I believe in the Lifegiver and all that he does, out of my belly is flowing rivers of living water, bubbling, and gurgling, and it resounds as a 'giggle'."

"Mother, are you happy to be in this time of your life?"

"Happy isn't the word to describe it. This is a joyous time. This time was ordained. Through you and your new queen, creation will be transformed!" She was getting excited.

"My Queen, I'm glad you mentioned my "queen" for I have a question for you." Anticipating his question, she leaned forward

Honey Is Where The Heart Is

with a gleam in her eyes,

"What is it, my King?" Y'nohe literally blushed.

"Do you know something of her, the one to be my queen?" The Queen, energized with immediate strength, sat straight up. Her color seemed to change before his eyes back to her lush black and yellow. There was nothing pale about her in that moment. She grasped her son by both arms and hugged him, squeezing him so tight that it surprised him.

"Do you know how long I've been waiting for you to ask this of me? I thought that I would see the Lifegiver before I could tell you what I know. But the Lifegiver said you had to believe in order to ask me. Your question tells me and Him that you believe." She stopped talking long enough to giggle. Her giggles sounded youthful like Nyohe's. He remembered his mother teaching him that the Lifegiver said,

'Except one be changed and become as a little child, one shall not enter His Kingdom.' She was getting closer and closer, so blindly trusting! But he liked hearing her this way. It reassured him that she was content. And the more she accepted her destiny, the better he could accept his. She shared,

"I had a dream long ago that my son would be king of our tribe. And in this dream, I walked into the Throne Room. You were in the Throne Room and there were two chairs, one for you and one for your queen. But it was odd. Instead of you and her sitting there, her chair was empty. You had removed your weapon, and you were defending her chair. As I continued to watch, her chair changed from its golden form to the color of a Breza." Contorting his face, Y'nohe interrupted,

"A Breza?"

"Yes, a Breza; striped black and white like a Breza. I've never seen you fight like this! You fought like one of my three special sentinels. Remember them? There was the one who lifted his weapon against eight hundred Spaws whom he slew at one time. And the one who fought until his hand was weary and cleaved unto his weapon; and then the one who stood his ground alone against the Noreths and had great victory. When I questioned what this all meant, the Lifegiver answered in my heart, 'your son is the champion to the One that shall lead with him at his side. He will know her by My 'divine design.' And then I woke up." The Queen was all smiles. She exhaled deeply. She felt she had laid aside the weight that had beset her. Even though she would not witness what was to come, she knew she had run her race that was set before her with patience.

The energy diminished. It burned out just as quickly as it had ignited. She again reclined onto her pedestal; free after releasing all she knew. Y'nohe stood there speechless. He had no response to what had been shared with him. His mind was reeling.

'What did all this mean?' he wondered to himself. He had no idea, but his mother seemed to believe the answer to his question was in her dream. He hoped she was right.

'And me fighting as a champion?' he thought. He had been well trained, but he could not imagine defeating one of their sentinels. Closing her eyes, the Queen was on her way to a restful sleep. He did not kneel beside her pedestal this time. Instead he took a step backward to allow her to rest. Abruptly the Queen reached out and firmly grabbed his hand. Slowly turning her head, she softly spoke,

"And don't worry about your brother. He will be fine. He knows more than you realize." Then her hand went limp again.

He walked out of the Throne Room backwards. After reaching the entrance, he turned and decided to fly back to the waxy chamber he had emerged from. He slowly retraced his path. Reflecting within himself, all he could think about was his mother's voice saying to him,

"Tribulation works patience and patience experience, and experience hope. And hope makes us not ashamed." His only hope at that moment was to be able to fall into a deep sleep when he reached that chamber. All he wanted right now was his mind to stop racing.

Narchom deliberately took his time unfurling his wings. Whenever he desired to spend time with the Lifegiver, he would enclose himself in his flyers. In that position he was reminded that

Honey Is Where The Heart Is

the Lifegiver transformed him into the beautiful creature he was now. He was amazed that presently he was orange and black, but before his transformation, he was yellow, black, and white striped. Allowing his wings to fall at his sides, he accidentally struck Charmon, waking her up.

"I would have just gotten up if you had asked me to," she smiled at him sleepily.

"I'm sorry. I didn't realize you were so near to me." He playfully stroked her flyer where he bumped her.

"You were in there for a while. Did you see or hear something from the Lifegiver?"

"Not only did I see something, but I have been sent by Him. I saw the Lifegiver sitting on His throne and above it stood His servants. It was the first time I had ever been that close to Him. I thought to myself, *'woe is me, for I am undone, because I am a Flutterby with unclean wings and I have seen the Lifegiver, the giver of life to all creation.'* One of His servants came up to me, and having what looked like mist in his hand, laid it upon my wings and said to me, "lo, this hath touched your wings and they have been given great strength." Then I heard the Lifegiver say, 'Whom shall I send, and who will go for us?' Then said I, "Here am I, send me."

And He said to me, "Go to every two-legged creature that spreads the flower dust and to every creeper on the ground who depends on the flower dust. Tell them when she takes her place as Queen, creation shall be like a tree planted by the rivers of water. That tree brings fruit in its season and its leaves will not wither and whatsoever fruit it bears shall be in abundance. So shall creation also!

Charmon could only stare at him. As he repeated the words of the Lifegiver, Narchom was engulfed in a light she had not seen before. It appeared as if a moonbeam and a sun ray had combined, bathing him in it from tip to tip. She could not feel her mouth moving, but yet, she could hear herself speaking,

"Don't tell me I can't go with you. For wherever you go I will go and wherever you lodge I will lodge. As the Lifegiver is your guide, He will be my guide. And if we lose our lives, where you die, I will die. The Lifegiver do so to me and more also if nothing but death separates us in this." Then as quickly as she had lost control of her own mouth, she regained it again. Seeing that she had made up her mind to go with him, Narchom did not try to convince her not to go.

"We must plan the way we need to go. We have many creatures to visit. The last thing the Lifegiver said to me was, 'Arise and eat, and then lay down again.' And then a second time, 'Arise and eat because the journey is a great one.'"

They both knew what they needed to do. They would have to leave the safety of their leafy cove to tell the good news to creation; the good news of the refreshing that would soon spread from creature to creature, from tree to tree, and from plant to plant. Needing to fill up on dew and flower dust, they headed out to do just that with Narchom leading the way.

Honey Is Where The Heart Is

CHAPTER TEN

"When are you going to tell your own offspring about 'him'?" Inol grilled Ilon. They had barely been speaking to each other lately. Watching his only offspring seem to lose all self-control, he missed the times when she respected him. He wondered if she loved him anymore. Her words were harsh, and her actions were caustic.

"Or should I say, tell 'him' about your offspring?"

'How did he know I hadn't told either of them,' she wondered to herself. Her elder's wisdom could be irritating at times, and now was not a time that she wanted to deal with him.

"You are not concerned that those dark, sinister creatures eat the young of those who are not their kind?" She turned her head. Determined that she would listen today, he walked over and stood in front of her. He peered into her eyes.

"Answer me!" he demanded. He was so close to her that she was unable to turn her head away.

"Why are you trying to live my life for me? I have everything under control, and I am not afraid of him hurting Noli. He cares too much for me to do that. I can handle this." Her elder just stared at her. She did not bat one eyelash. They were in a stare down, and neither of them was going to budge. His obstinate character matched her stubbornness.

Lino had been watching the two of them for a moment. She disliked the fact that her tribe seemed to be falling apart. The only thing she could do lately was try to be the peacekeeper. She pretended to walk in on them suddenly.

"Oh Inol, I was looking for you. I need your help with something. Do you have time?" At first, he did not speak or move. He did not want to lose this stare down. Finally turning to his mate, he said,

"Yes, I'm done here. What do you need?" and walked away, leaving Ilon sitting there, still staring straight ahead. She stood to all fours, head held high, and walked out of the lair. When he reached his mate's side, he sadly asked,

"Why is she doing this? What could she possibly be thinking?" Lino was silent. She gingerly bit her lip.

"What is it? If you have something to say, say it," he complained. "Why not?" he continued, pointing towards the entrance, "she talks to me any way she wants to."

"My place isn't to disrespect you, but to bring honor to you. I can't help but wonder, what if you just tell her the truth? Tell her what really happened that day." It took all the strength he could muster for the tears not to flow from his saddened eyes. Clearing the lump from his throat, he whimpered a reply,

"I can't. The Lifegiver promised He would send me a sign to let me know when to tell her. I can't go against what He said. I must continue to trust Him. How can I tell her to trust and believe in Him if I don't?"

Lino could see the obvious anguish in his face. She desired the tribal life they had before that eventful day. But she had to trust the Lifegiver, too. Knowing that she could not take away the pain he was feeling, she had to believe that all things work together for the good of those who love the Lifegiver. She had to remind herself the 'things' her tribe was experiencing was no different. Leaning against Inol's side, Lino purred,

"I am here." He exhaled, deeply. He genuinely appreciated her. It was times like this that he needed his mate right where she was, at his side.

Honey Is Where The Heart Is

Forgetting where he was for a moment, Y'nohe quickly sat up in the chamber. He remembered that he had returned to slow down his racing thoughts. The quiet moment calmed him somewhat and his rest brought clarity. Realizing how occupied he was trying to forget what was going on with the Queen, he remembered he had not shared with Nyohe about their mother.

"What will I say to him? I must consult the Queen on this." When he spoke out loud, he experienced an encouragement translated in his heart,

"No, you are the King," then silence. Y'nohe froze. Trying to determine what just happened, he quieted himself. His wings were not buzzing. His antennae were still. He even held his breath. Focusing on nothing, he heard it again,

"You are the King. Wisdom rests on you. Talk to him. If you need Me, I will tell you what to say."

Involuntary tears fell from his cheek onto his lap. His mother had taught him that the Lifegiver interacts with kings in authority so that they may lead a quiet and peaceable life in humility. They just had to be willing to hear whatever truth He spoke to them. It was the Lifegiver who gives wisdom unto the wise and knowledge to them that show understanding. Knowing that it was the Lifegiver who removes and sets up kings, the reality of him being King could not be denied.

Y'nohe's smile broke through his tears. He headed off in the direction of what the younger Eebs called the "bumble room.' It was a compartment designated for them to run and chase one other around and have fun. Since they were not allowed out of the Palace alone, they entertained each other in this area. The nearer Y'nohe came to the bumble room, he wondered if the Lifegiver was causing an unforeseen circumstance to become known to them.

Standing at the entrance, he watched the younger Eebs buzzing about, socializing among themselves. Even in his playful mode, Nyohe demonstrated agility and precision in his movements.

Y'nohe was impressed by his younger brother's physical abilities and his wisdom. He possessed an abundance of knowledge that accentuated his understanding.

Y'nohe stepped into the bumble room. Instinctively, every Eeb in his presence came to a halt. They all bowed. They waited for him to release them. Except Nyohe, of course. He ran up to Y'nohe and threw his arms around him, hugging him tightly.

"Hey, you here to have some fun today?" he grinned, allowing his elder brother to breathe only for a moment before he embraced him again.

"Not today. We need to talk." Freeing himself from his younger brother's grip, he turned to the others commanding, "you may go." The other Eebs filed out of the bumble room single file. As they walked by him, a few of them bowed their head again out of respect for their King. Nyohe smiled. He was so proud of his elder. Once they were alone, Y'nohe's demeanor changed. Exhaling deeply, he relaxed. The elder could now concentrate on the younger. He could not help but notice the expression on Nyohe's face. Crossing his arms, Y'nohe inquired,

"And what are you smiling about?" Smiling was becoming contagious. Chuckling, Nyohe replied,

"Nothing, your Majesty!"

Too late; the contagion was now infectious. The two brothers laughed in abandon. It was such a freeing moment for Y'nohe. With his wee body carrying so much stress the past few weeks, this encounter released a great deal of it.

"What do you want to talk to me about?"

'When did this younger one mature so suddenly without me noticing his transformation?' Y'nohe thought, "I know you've already noticed that our Queen, our mother is weak right now. She is in preparation for..." He hesitated, seeking to find the right words. No sooner than he hesitated, he remembered what the Lifegiver had spoken to him earlier. He continued to speak, trusting that the words were not just his own,

"She is awaiting the Lifegiver so that this tribe can live its purpose. When I become King, a great change will take place." Again, Nyohe beamed.

'Why is he so calm? Even I couldn't digest all that the Queen shared with me?" pondered the elder one, "Okay Nyohe, you know

Honey Is Where The Heart Is

something. What is it? Have you been listening outside the Throne Room again?" Laughing, the younger one responded,

"No, I haven't. Not lately anyway. The Queen discovered me the last time I tried that. She taught me a lesson that day! She had me clean all the servants' wings, showing them that I serve them too. Do you know how many wings that is?" They laughed together. Y'nohe finally asked,

"How are you calm? Do you realize that our Queen is dying?"

"Yes, I do. Before she had the chance to tell me what was happening, I had a dream. When I shared it with her, she told me the truth."

"A dream? Can you share it with me?" Since one of the compartments in the wall was large enough for them both, Nyohe motioned for his elder brother to join him in it. They entered it and sat across from each other, getting comfortable in the snug hideaway.

"I remember it like it was yesterday. I knew this dream was different from the other ones; not only did it stay in my mind, it found its way to my heart."

"What do you mean by 'this dream.'? Do you dream a lot?"

"What do you mean by 'a lot'? I dream all the time. Don't you?" Y'nohe shook his head. His younger brother had his undivided attention. He was more intrigued now than before.

"It was one of those nights that Mother buzzed me to sleep; or so I thought it was her. I walked into the Throne Room. It was brighter than usual. All I could hear was bzz, bzz, bzz. The buzz got louder and louder, like all of us together. But instead of being the sound of thousands of Eebs, it was someone singing. I was mesmerized by this voice. It was so clear and eloquent. It tinkled, like when it rains and the rain patters on our Palace. Now the odd thing was, when I walked into the Throne Room, the throne was turned backwards. I could hear a voice but not see anyone. And from the throne flowed the most beautiful honey I'd ever seen! It wasn't gold like ours but translucent, almost clear! But it was so beautiful! And I realized that the light in the Palace was coming from this honey. As I stood there watching, this honey that had flowed from the throne, began to cover everything in the room, even me. It was warm and engulfing! It covered me completely and can you believe it wasn't sticky?"

"Not sticky?"

"Not at all. The experience was incredible. I stood stationary in that spot not able to move. I knew what would happen and it did. The throne began to pivot slowly around. Somehow, I knew that our Queen wasn't there. I held my breath waiting to see who it was. And she was beautiful! Even her wings shimmered! Her face is the only thing I can't remember! But you know what was amazing?" Nyohe paused. Y'nohe could only shake his head. Not only was his brother growing up before his eyes, but he was doing an excellent job recreating his dream.

"She wasn't the same color as we are. She was…"

"Black and white?" he interjected. Nyohe was surprised by his brother's response.

"How'd you know that?"

"Something mother shared with me." Y'nohe was more confident than ever that what was to come, was meant to be. He grabbed his younger brother by the shoulders, looked him in his eyes, and said,

"This is the day that the Lifegiver has made. Let us rejoice and be glad in it!"

CHAPTER ELEVEN

"Mepaw, where are we going…in the dark?" Noli asked his elder nervously.

"It's okay. I go out in the night all the time. Besides, you are with me. Don't I always protect you?" she asked him. She playfully batted him with one of her huge front paws. Grabbing at her paw, he momentarily forgot his fear. "It's a surprise. You'll see. Look up there. Isn't it beautiful?" She turned his attention to the full moon, glaring and beaming back at them. There were plenty of shadows tonight. The moon provided the perfect stage for them.

Inol watched them when they both walked out of the lair. Consumed by distress, he tired of being angry with his offspring. There was nothing more he could say to her. Hoping wisdom had taken root somehow, he had planted every seed of wisdom imaginable in her mind. Staring out after them until their forms disappeared into the night, he sighed deeply.

"Please bring them back safely to me," he prayed under his breath. He closed his eyes and leaned his massive head forward. The thick swirls of hair about his head created a personal cove where he could be alone, just him and the Lifegiver. He did not try to say a word. He simply let the tears flow. Holding them back had become difficult.

Ilon and Noli continued their way through the tall grass. It was a cool night and the wind was still. Noli's nose, though immature, caught whiff of something. Sensing danger, he trampled on his elder's feet, trying to get as close to her as he could.

"Mepaw, what's that smell?"

"No need to be afraid. It's a friend," she explained, smiling at him. Her expression changed quickly. She sniffed into the air, raising her huge head to get a better whiff. Crouching down onto all fours, she growled low and deep. She placed Noli behind her to protect him, then turned to face the aggressor.

"Show yourself," she spoke forcefully into the dark. As he watched from behind his elder's hind leg. Noli's eyes widened in fear. The shadow emerged out of the tall grass. Its eyes were blood red and it was so dark that it mingled with the night. The tail on its end twitched and pulsed.

"You must be Ilon. I see why my brother is taken with you. Even your little one casts an aroma," he laughed menacingly. Ilon did not move a muscle. She kept her piercing, golden eyes on the dark thing standing before her. But she did not understand the color of his eyes. He seemed to be the same as Napreth, but his eyes were of a different color, of a different nature. Not only was the hair on the back of her neck upright, but every hair on her entire body.

'Did he take a step towards us,' she thought to herself. Noli's tiny claws were gripping her tighter and tighter. If she could smell her young ones' fear, so could he. Finally speaking, she asked it a question,

"Who are you and how do you know my name?" Anpreth chuckled.

"You've been spending all this time with my elder brother and he not once mentioned me? I wonder why?" Now he was teasing. A horrid odor filled her nostrils. He smelled nothing like Napreth.

'Why is he giving off this scent?' she wondered, *'it's not fear, but something else.'* She remembered smelling this before. The moment was so intense she could not recall when or where. He spoke again,

"And what's really amazing to me is that he didn't mention

Honey Is Where The Heart Is

your young one. You know it's not always safe out here in the dark," As quickly as he appeared, he was gone. She did not remember blinking her eyes, but she must have. He disappeared and she had missed his exit.

Noli pulled on his mother's tail. She had stretched it out, waiting to attack if necessary. She turned to look at the young one.

"Can we go now? Can we see the surprise tomorrow?" Only for an instant did she let her guard down.

"Yes, we can go," she responded, relaxing her body a little more. He was still frightened. Sitting down on her rear haunches to allow her passenger aboard, she asked him,

"Want to ride instead?"

"That will be fun!" he said and climbed onto her back. She stood to all fours and allowed him to nestle behind her head. He got comfortable quickly. As they neared home, he broke the silence,

"Mepaw, was that one of the creatures that Grand One told me about?" Recollecting the stories her elder had shared with her when she was his age, she remembered the day that she interrupted her elder telling Noli the same story. In her mind, she could hear her elder's voice clearly,

'And they did one thing that the Lifegiver did not like. They ate their own young,' his masculine voice echoing louder, *and if they ate their own young, what would they do to hers?* This was the topic of conversation she had with herself the rest of the way home.

Honey Is Where The Heart Is

CHAPTER TWELVE

Charmon could barely keep up with him. She had never seen him fly so strongly, and with such purpose. Their mission was to talk to as many creepy crawly things as they could, and to share with the other Flutterbys and the two-legged flying creatures too. Narchom had his mind set on doing what he was told. He believed he could do all things through the Lifegiver who strengthened him. As they started out on their journey, all he could think about was the last thing the Lifegiver said to them. He said,

"Go and tell creation that its restoration is at hand. Take neither flower or dust, nor petals, nor food for your journey. And whatever clan you abide with, there you stay until it's time for you to move on. When you come into another tribe, bless them if they are worthy so that peace may come upon them." Narchom remembered every word verbatim.

They fluttered non-stop. Charmon wondered if they would have any life left in them when their journey was complete. But if they did not, their lives would be worth the sacrifice. Knowing the Lifegiver would help her to understand, she was neither confused nor afraid. She set her face like flint, believing no matter what happened, she would not regret a moment.

First, they visited the Tarcaprilles. Some were brown, some yellow, and some bright green. Many of them were multicolored, furry, and with many legs. They encountered them just in time. The Tarcaprilles were about to enter their secret hideaways where the Lifegiver transformed them into Flutterbys. To the Tarcaprilles he said,

"The Lifegiver knows your work, your labor, and your patience. Because you have overcome, during the restoration of creation, you will eat of the Tree of Life which flourishes where the Lifegiver rests."

Next, he traveled to the Letebes. They were of the strongest of the creeping crawling things. Their divided compartments on their backs ranged in a variety of colors. Charmon encountered one of the most beautiful of the Letebes, having a red back with black spots on it. To the Letebes, Narchom said,

"The Lifegiver knows your works, and tribulations, and poverty, but you are really rich. Fear none of the things that you will suffer, but instead be faithful. Dur- ing the restoration of creation, you will overcome even death."

By the time they reached the Lyfs, Charmon was exhausted. Allowing her to rest, Narchom met with them alone. He had forgotten how the Lyfs did not sit still long. He grew tired just by watching them. Their tiny bodies with their huge eyes within an eye were always moving about looking for a bit of food to get into. To the Lyfs he said,

"The Lifegiver knows your works and sees where you live. He knows that you hold fast to His name and have not denied Him. But He has a few things against you. You allow some of your kind to believe in the teaching of the Spaws; some- times to eat the flesh of others instead of the fruit provided. Turn away from this so that during the restoration of creation, you will eat of the food from where the Lifegiver dwells. And He has a gift for you; a white stone with the name of your kind on it, so that your kind is always remembered." After the Lyfs, Narchom himself was exhausted. By the time he returned to Charmon, he could barely stay awake. Charmon suggested,

"Narchom, you've done so much over the past few days.

Honey Is Where The Heart Is

How about you rest tomorrow in order to renew your strength?" He did not argue with her. He was so tired that as soon as he curled his black and orange flyers around himself and his mate, he was fast asleep. As for Charmon, she was safe in his flyers. It was so peaceful that she felt as if she was dwelling in the Lifegiver's secret place.

With every step he took in hope, his weakened body seemed to move in a new strength. He had walked a long way and yet, still did not know why he was on this path. Nothing was familiar to him. Although had never been this way before, he knew which way to go. The only thing he remembered hearing was,

"Get yourself out of this country and from your kind and go into a land that I will show you. And you will be made into a great tribe and you will be blessed, your name will be great, and you will be a blessing to others."

Every day he survived on those words, if only he could eat them. He desired to eat but could not. Hunger weakened his body but sharpened his mind. His thoughts were precise and clear. The only thing he wanted besides food was a deep river to wade in. Caked upon his body were layers of days-old dirt. He could no longer tell his true color, but he knew beneath the filth was the glory of the Lifegiver. Normally he would clean himself, but his tongue was dry from lack of water. As for the shroud of hair about his head, it became matted after his second day of walking. If he could only get clean…

Drip. Drip. Drip. She watched as the raindrops rolled over the edge of the violet's petals. Though she loved the rain, she had to be careful in it. Getting caught in the rain could cause her wings to stick together. Without her wings operating properly, she would be

without flight. The inability to fly would be like cutting off her life source. Enhoy was grateful for many things in her life, especially the joy of spreading the flower dust. Flying allowed her to help the flowers be fruitful and multiply.

     Even though she could not fly and use them today, she loved her wings. They allowed her to soar above creation. She loved to look down and see all of nature's hues. But the true desire of her heart was the ability to make honey. Even though the maturity for her to do so not come yet, she could feel the gift stirring. Anticipation was her motivation. It was getting harder to wait but she knew she had to. She was alone, no community to bond with. She had not forsaken the purpose of assembling together with her kind. Her desire was to be part of a community so she could encourage others. Enhoy enjoyed caring for others and could not wait to get the chance to serve.

CHAPTER THIRTEEN

As soon as Ilon walked into her presence, she noticed that Lino was annoyed. Lino just sat there. She did not turn and look at her or speak. She was irritated by her offspring's actions. It was Ilon's choice to start the conversation.

"Have you seen Noli this morning?" she asked in a hushed voice. Choosing her words carefully, Lino clenched her teeth, her jaw muscles tightened.

"Haven't you? From what I've heard you promised to always protect him. I don't understand why my little one is curled up in a ball beside his Grand One still frightened from last night!" Her voice heightened an octave with each word that she spat out at her offspring.

Ilon, in all her years, had never witnessed anger in this elder. Even when hunting, she did not express anger but instead skill and might. But this was different. She was mad. It bothered her to see this elder upset like this. Her intentions were not to hurt them, but just to live as she pleased. Wishing she had a bushy mass on her head that could fall about her face, Ilon lowered her head and nestled it on a paw.

"He will be fine. He just hasn't been exposed to…"

"What is wrong with you?" Lino sternly asked, walking towards her, "exposed to what? Something that wants to devour him?"

"You are just exaggerating to try to prove a point," she rebutted without looking at her elder.

"Do you not remember the stories your elder shared with you when you were young yourself?" Lino realized her emotions were getting the best of her. She tried to calm down.

"He only told me those things to entertain himself," She chuckled trying to change the mood. It did not work. Lino was determined for her to see how serious the situation was.

"It wasn't for entertainment as you think. It was an instruction from the Lifegiver to teach these words to our offspring and talk about it when we sit, when we walk, when we lie down, and when we get up. But I guess you've for- gotten a lot of things since you have seemed to have forgotten which kind you are!" Her elder was relentless. Lino's mind was made up not lose any more battles!

"You know I can take care of myself and Noli. I wasn't afraid."

"But he was, and you should have been too! He told me how the eyes of that beast were red." Ilon remembered how red his eyes had become. They caught her off guard because she expected them to be yellow as the sun and because she expected it to be Napreth. Ilon's blank look on her face confirmed for Lino her assumptions were correct. She did not remember the significance of his red eyes.

"He had an odor, didn't he?"

"How did you know that?"

"And it wasn't their usual one of "them" smell, but it was more like rotted flesh." Lino's description brought back the smell of the stench to her nostrils.

"When they crave the flesh of a young one, they are overtaken by the sensation to feed on their innocent flesh. The desire is so strong that their eyes turn red, as if the blood of their kill has filled their eyes. They will fight their own to get to the flesh. He was concentrating on Noli and he would have killed you to get to him." Ilon was stunned. Saying nothing, she thought to herself,

'How did I forget that part?'

"Did you tell your mate, that other kind, that Noli even

Honey Is Where The Heart Is

existed? "Again, Ilon remained silent, her thoughts racing.

'Why haven't I told him? Is it because I no longer have the Lifegiver's love in my heart?' Had He given her thoughts over to a reprobate mind, causing her to do things against her nature?

A single tear rolled down her smooth-haired face, the start of a deluge. This was not her usual tears of anger and frustration, but sorrow instead. For sorrow from the Lifegiver worked to bring change to her heart. When the dam broke, it released a flood of emotions. Her sobs softened Lino's heart. She embraced Ilon, licking the tears from her face. They sat together in silence. The Lifegiver used Lino to comfort Ilon who had once been inconsolable; but not anymore. A clean heart was created, and a right spirit renewed in her. The change her elders anticipated had come. They had waited on the Lifegiver and now Ilon's compassion had been replenished.

Honey Is Where The Heart Is

CHAPTER FOURTEEN

Slowly opening her eyes Charmon awakened first. With her head on his chest, she could hear every thump-thump of Narchom's tiny but strong life source. His heart seemed to beat in unison with his thoughts of the Lifegiver. Though her mate loved her deeply every day, she knew the love he had for the Lifegiver was eternal. Initially she was concerned that he would choose the Lifegiver first over her, but as she came to know the Lifegiver for herself, she realized that it was not a choice to be made. They both learned that when blessed with a mate, the Lifegiver enhances the relationship making the them both better for each other.

She wanted to let Narchom sleep but could not. She knew she had to wake him because they had to do a lot of traveling today. They had been obedient and had sought out the Tarcaprilles, the Lyfs, and the Letebes but today they had to speak to the two-leggeds, the Dribs. Sometimes she was envious of them. Not resentful, but covetous of their gifts. The Dribs' wings allowed them to fly higher and much faster, while the Flutterbys' fliers only gave them flight. Still Charmon was grateful for her ability to fly. To her, flying was better than being glued to the ground. She thanked the Lifegiver for the ability. Narchom still had her snuggled inside of his flyers.

"Narchom," she gently shook him, "Narchom, we have to get ready." First, he stretched out his legs then his flyers. She watched as he allowed them to unfurl slowly and then snap into place, full color, crisp, and ready to fly! Well, not fly, but more flutter.

"Good morning beautiful? Did I mention that I just love your colors?"

"Yes, only thousands of times. I wonder why?" They both laughed, since she was the exact same color as he, only a shade darker.

"But I do have some good news. The Lifegiver's timing is perfect. He has called together the two-leggeds to meet today. He has shown me their location and He is sending us there to speak to them. He always provides all the time we need!" Although Narchom had just opened his eyes, he was excited already. Since their travels would be light, they neither ate nor drank that morning. Deciding to find food on the way, they headed out to find the Dribs.

As they fluttered along, Charmon recognized where they were. She had been to this place before. It was a secluded grove of tall trees, visited by only a few creatures. The Dribs called it their Sanctuary. They heard the two-legged ones before they could see them. The group was up high in the trees. At such a height, they could safely meet without having to set a watchman for their enemies. Not many creatures on the ground ascended this high into the trees. Narchom and Charmon rested on one of the branches. He leaned over to her and yelled,

"How will we get their attention?" To Charmon the chattering was so loud he sounded as if he whispered.

"I don't know," she screamed back, "I don't think they realize we are here!"

Suddenly a strong gust blew through the Sanctuary. The wind settled in the top of the tree where the two Flutterbys had settled. The Lifegiver created a great noise that caught the attention of the two-leggeds. When they heard the sound in the top of the tree, they all turned to see what caused it. There on a branch were two Flutterbys. Surprised, the crowd went silent. Since he now had their attention, Narchom began to speak,

Honey Is Where The Heart Is

"Consider the lives of all the two-leggeds. You neither sow nor reap and have not a storehouse. Yet the Lifegiver feeds you. And as He cares for you, He also cares for creation. What I have to say to you today, He is sharing with you because you help to spread the precious flower dust. This day, the Lifegiver has sent me to tell you that it is time for the restoration of creation. And as you wait and hope for it, He reminds us that sometimes, deferred hope makes the heart sick. To remain encouraged, He wants you to focus on how He uniquely designed your kind and that there's no others as yourself!" He began without hesitating or taking a moment to catch his breath,

"So to you, the clan of the Edvo, the Lifegiver says that you are without spot or blemish. You are not without color; He colored you white. He wants you to remember just as He designed you pure white, creation will be purified." A unified 'coo' rose into the atmosphere as all the Edvos thanked the Lifegiver. Charmon smiled, watching Narchom speak. She enjoyed listening to him when he used the Lifegiver's words to encourage others. Then to the yellow Dribs with the black wings he declared,

"To you Leorio tribe, the Lifegiver says where you live is your reminder. The ability to create the unique place where you lay your young ones is a gift from Him. Your homes are deep and shaped like wells; a well that can supply water to those who thirst. Remember that creation will drink again, replenished in the restoration." Another chorus of chirps expressed how thankful the Leorio clan was to be included in this moment. Turning his attention to the Nusdrib, he noticed they were yellow-chested, with brightly colored bodies and short wings. Though their wings were short, they could fly extremely fast, and they were able to feed easily from the flowers with their curved bills. Narchom smiled as he spoke,

"The Lifegiver smiles upon you, oh great Nusdrib! He has blessed you with being able to draw deep from the flowers. He lets you taste and see that what He has created is good! Your bill will remind you that what He speaks is sweeter than honey within the honeycomb. When creation is restored, it will taste sweeter than it ever has before." The Nusdrib could not sit still any longer. They were so encouraged by his words that they lifted from the branch and encircled Narchom and Charmon, creating a multi-colored funnel around them. Once they calmed themselves, they returned to their stationary position.

Though engrossed in the excitement of his mission, Narchom maintained his own composure. He was delighted and his heart was glad! Anxiously, the Ch'fin waited their turn. They all wondered what the Lifegiver had given to them as a reminder. To the Ch'fin he exclaimed,

"Sing unto the Lifegiver a new song. Your songs are a continual blessing to Him! Your reminder? Your voices! So, lift up your voices even higher to encourage yourself. Let them resound loud, clear, and long! You are also seed eaters and when those seeds are sown, creation reaps in restoration!"

Although they were few in number, the Ch'fin sounded like the voices of the Lifegiver's servants about His throne. The chirps of rejoicing echoed on the wind. Enjoying their praise, Narchom did not interrupt them. Finally, they were able to quiet themselves. Narchom then turned his attention to the last group of Dribs.

Being the smallest of all the two-leggeds, they were very petite in size. The Drimmumbigh moved so quickly that their wings seemed to disappear. And as they flapped them, a soft vibrating noise was created, almost like a hum.

"You, Drimmumbigh are the only ones of the two-leggeds that can fly backwards. And as easily as you can fly backwards, the Lifegiver will quickly bring the restoration forward! It will come, for yet a little while, and will not tarry! Wait for it for it is closer than you know!"

By now, even Charmon could not contain her excitement! Another strong gust of wind swept through the Sanctuary and remained in the tops of the trees. The Dribs that surrounded the Flutterbys were all different, yet they began to tweet, chirp, and peep in unison. Charmon was amazed and she marveled at the sight. Without the Lifegiver's decision for her to be at Narchom's side, she would not have been here on this day. She was grateful that the Lifegiver had chosen her to be his mate.

CHAPTER FIFTEEN

Inol inhaled deeply. He recognized her scent as soon as she walked in. Thinking he was asleep, she quietly walked over to where he was laying, and sat behind him. He was sprawled comfortably on his right side, his strong legs stretched out from his massive body. She moved to lay on her left side, placing her head on his left shoulder. Her plan was to just lay there until he awoke. He was surprised by her actions.

"Ilon, you're headed out tonight?" he asked her, purposely removing any traces of sarcasm in his question.

"I thought you may have been asleep," she paused, took a deep breath, then continued, "yes, I am going but I wanted to talk to you first." Even though she did not see the surprise in his face, Inol could not help but to wrinkle his brow.

"Talk to me? About what?" Emotion swelling to a lump in her throat, she bit her lip to hold back the oncoming tears.

"I just wanted to come and tell you that I am so sorry for how I've been treating you lately. I'm sorry for hurting your feelings. I'm sorry for the way I've been speaking to you. I'm sorry for…" He interrupted her,

"All I needed was the first 'I'm sorry.'" His smile in the dark replaced the wrinkled brow. Feeling moisture on his back, he turned his head to look at his offspring. She was looking directly at him. Ilon wanted him to see her tears. She was not hiding them anymore.

"I'm sorry, Mepaw." She had not called him that since she was young. He remembered the times she rode on the back of his neck, hanging on to his hairy head. He thought about the many times she pounced on his swollen belly. She was so in- nocent then and he loved her so much. All he wanted to do, then and now, was protect his sweet, little one.

"No more sorrys. I could never stop loving you, no matter how you have treated me." She reached across his body and playfully ran her full-size paw through the thick coarse hair around his head.

"Mepaw," she whispered.

"Yes?"

"I love you," She snuggled her head against his shoulder. Now it was his turn to let the tears fall.

"And I love you too," he paused, "I thought you had to go?"

"Oh, I do, but I just want to sit here with you a little longer." He repositioned his head back onto the ground. Knowing now that her heart was changing, his desire was to be here for her if she needed him for comfort.

"My Lords, my Lords, the Queen calls for you," the servant informed, trying to wake them up. Y'nohe opened his eyes. Realizing he was still in the bumble room, he recognized Nyohe in another chamber also still asleep.

"Wake up Nyohe, wake up," Y'nohe urged, shaking his younger brother, "Get up. Mother, I mean, the Queen wants us." Nyohe stretched out his legs from inside the chamber and then slid the rest of his body out. He hovered for a moment to wake himself up. Once he planted himself on the waxy floor, Y'nohe turned to his mother's servant and asked,

Honey Is Where The Heart Is

"Do we need to fly, or can we walk?"

"The Queen says you can walk," she answered and was silent again. She was about to fly off to get back to the Queen, when Y'nohe stopped her.

"Wait, walk with us." She had a look of immediate resistance on her face.

"My Lord, but I must return to the Queen. And I am merely a servant; to walk with my Lords in this way, I cannot." Nyohe asked,

"What is your name?" She froze in mid-step.

"What's wrong?" he asked, "Don't you know your name?" She did not respond. The only other person who ever asked her name was her Queen. She had been trained to serve, and she believed that was her purpose.

"Yes, I know my name, but why does my Lord need to know my name? I am just a servant." She lowered her head in such humility, impressing the two standing before her. Y'nohe's demeanor changed, his kingly character witnessed by the confidence in his voice,

"From now on, I call you not a servant, but my friend. For a servant knows not what their Lord does, and as I take my position as King, I will need your help. You have served my mother well and I will need you also for my Queen. In order to call you friend, I must know your name." Nyohe and the servant stood there in amazement. Nyohe spoke first,

"Wow Y'nohe, I mean, my Lord," and he bowed his head out of respect. He witnessed the mantle of this kingdom fall upon his brother's shoulders.

"My Lord," she spoke, raising her head in assurance "my name is Hyeon and it is an honor to serve you; and also to be a friend of yours and your Queen."

"Good. Now let us fly the rest of the way to meet our Queen."

The three of them hovered for a moment. Then Y'nohe took the lead, followed by Nyohe and following was Hyeon. The change had already begun.

Inol inhaled deeply. He recognized her scent as soon as she walked in. Knowing that he was awake, she quickly walked over to where he was laying and sat down near his stomach. He was still lying on his right side, his legs stretched out, his huge paws turned up. She laid her body out on the ground, mimicking his position. She placed her head on his foreleg and quietly spoke,

"Today has been a long day. It's good to have some peace. Noli finally went to sleep and everyone else is out. Did she come to see you?" Lino asked.

"Yes, she did, and I must say, she seems to have changed overnight. It is true when the Lifegiver says that a little child shall lead them. I understand how the love of your child can change your life."

"When are you going to tell her?"

"Not yet. I wait on the Lifegiver. He told me He would give me a sign. I must keep trusting Him. His timing is perfect."

"I know, but we have been waiting so long for you to tell her. I hope it will be soon." Lino closed her eyes for the first time in days. Out of concern for her tribe, he had not been sleeping well. Knowing all she had to do was continue to trust the Lifegiver was one aspect but waiting to see the change was another. Trusting could be hard to do sometimes. He had always been there for them when He was needed, so no need to stop trusting Him now. After a few moments, Inol heard the sound he had been anticipating. Lifting his massive head, he looked at his mate. Lino had finally drifted off to sleep, purring ever so lightly. He smiled. He did not mind her purring tonight. At least Inol knew she was getting some rest.

CHAPTER SIXTEEN

Napreth was not hiding in the shadows tonight. He was out waiting in the open for Ilon. She was surprised to see him in the clearing.

"I've been waiting for you. What took you so long?" he asked impatiently, pacing back and forth.

"There was something I needed to do before I came." Sensing his irritability, she asked, "what's wrong? You seem upset." She sat down in the clearing and watched him walk to and fro. Not wanting to sound emotional, he intentionally spoke slowly.

"Upset isn't the right word. Confused maybe. Why didn't you tell me you had a little one?" He tried to stop pacing but could not. His frustration would not let him. Even his erratic tail movements demonstrated how irritated he was. Not answering his question, she asked him,

"So that was your brother. How did he know where we meet? And what were the red eyes about?" Napreth did not answer either. It was not that he did not know the answer. He hoped instead that he would not have this issue with her. No offspring, no problem. He stopped pacing and sat a few feet from her.

"I told him about you. I had to meet your elders, didn't I? So, you needed to meet my brother. I didn't know he was going there alone though. But still, he informs me you have a young one." She did not respond.

'Why didn't I tell him?' she thought. She was uncertain of her own actions. She loved Noli and was proud of him. But when she was around Napreth, she pushed her offspring to the back of her mind. Ilon noticed that although Napreth had stopped pacing, he was keeping his distance. He sat down but was not sitting near her.

"I don't know why I didn't tell you about him, about Noli," she explained," he's young and he means everything to me. He is all I have to remind me of..." She stopped herself in midsentence.

"Remind you of what? Or should I say who? Why don't you talk about what happened?"

Standing to all fours, he moved towards her. She watched him as he neared. Tonight, he did not seem as dangerous. Tonight, he was not mysterious. Tonight... maybe she should just leave. But not yet. She had to know for herself about the red eyes. Just as he got close enough for their whiskers to touch, she slightly turned her head, purposely avoiding his contact.

"Tell me about your brother's eyes. I've never seen your eyes red like that. What was it?" Napreth was quiet. He had to tell her. He was too entangled now not to tell her the truth. Finding what he thought would be the right words, he began to speak,

"I confess when I first met you, I was glad to notice you didn't have any offspring with you. Our kind at one time was plentiful. And then the famine came; nothing to eat in sight anywhere. Out of desperation," he hesitated, "to survive we began to eat our own young ones; only the ones who were sick and dying. And then as the rains came and the land flourished again, our kind increased in number," again he paused, "but it was too late. We had tasted the blood of innocent ones and wanted more," he lowered his voice, "so then we began to eat the young of other kinds."

Ilon's whole body tensed. She bolted up straight. She replayed the previous scenario in her mind. Now that she was thinking clearly, she realized that his brother's focus had been on Noli. She fixated on Napreth as he continued.

"The blood of an innocent one smells differently from that of an aged one. You don't understand. We can smell their blood.

Honey Is Where The Heart Is

The desire to kill and eat them, blinds us. Our eyes go red because our desire takes us over." Ilon focused on Napreth's face as he explained.

'Did his eyes just change colors?' she wondered, *'Was that a glimmer of red I just saw even just from him speaking about it?'* and then asked, "You do that too?"

"It's what I am, Ilon. I can't not be what I am. Besides it's not our fault," he answered gruffly, turning his head away from her.

"What do you mean it's not your fault? You chose to do that. Desire doesn't take you over. You give into it. Just like I chose to be your mate when I know it's wrong." She said it so quickly that it startled her. Frustrated, Napreth retorted,

"If you want to be my mate and I want to be yours why is that not right? How is being my mate so wrong? How can I have a choice in something that I cannot control?" Since having that moment with her Mepaw, Ilon's perspective about her life was constantly changing. She stood to her paws.

"We are not of the same kind, that's why. The Lifegiver didn't intend for us to be together. We are not equally yoked." She even surprised herself, thinking,

'Did I just admit that the Lifegiver was right about something?'

"What do you know about the Lifegiver?' Napreth yelled. Ilon was irritated. Not only was she seeing a side of him that she didnot approve of, but he was raising his voice at her without cause.

"What do I know about the Lifegiver?" she stated, "He gives life to all creation, and it's our choice to live it in such a way that pleases Him!" Again, she was caught off guard by her own words.

"Life! What kind of life is it that I can't enjoy what I like? What I want? He tricked us! He let us eat the innocents then He punished us for doing it!" Napreth turned and walked away from her.

Ilon reminisced for a moment. She remembered everything her elders had told her about the Lifegiver. She remembered that He chastised those He loved. She remembered that He provided for all He created. And the most important thing she remembered in her moment of clarity was that the Lifegiver would not let her be tempted far beyond what she could handle. Instead He would make a way for her to escape; to get out of it. She recognized this was her Lifegiver granting her the chance not to do something she would regret later. Ilon sensed a calming affect wash over her.

"You know Napreth, I am sure the Lifegiver warned you and your kind about the innocents. And He probably gave you a way not to do it, but you didn't choose that. But instead, you proceeded in the way you wanted instead of seeing your desire would lead you the wrong way. Well, I'm not going to do that. Right here, right now, the Lifegiver is giving me a way out, and I am taking it." She turned to walk away. Napreth, in his anger, grabbed her by her shoulder, his claws digging into her golden coat. Emitting a roar of her own, she quickly turned her head, and plunged her sharp teeth into his paw. He snatched his paw away in pain. Now facing him, Ilon locked eyes with him, battle ready.

"Do you think you will be able to just walk away from me? Do you know who I am? I am Napreth!" he screamed, standing there in the clearing licking his bitten paw.

"Yes, I know who you are. You are one of 'them'." Then she spun around and walked away into the night, heading home to her own kind.

CHAPTER SEVENTEEN

It was dark by the time Narchom and Charmon left the secret grove of trees. They were pleasantly exhausted. The unending celebration between the different two-legged tribes lasted longer than they anticipated. Honestly, they had not known what to expect.

"We have to find a place to rest for the night. It is too dark for us to continue on our way," Narchom explained, "besides, I am tired and getting sleepy. Even my flyers are moving slowly."

"How about a warm cubby hole in the side of a tree?"

"That would be nice. Let's look for one." They separated only for a moment, each looking on opposite sides of trees. Charmon could barely flutter her flyers. How glad she was when she heard Narchom call out,

"Found one! Perfect size for just the two of us!" She tried following the sound of his voice. Looking from side to side in the dark, she searched for him but still did not see him.

"Where are you?" she asked,

"I'm right here," he responded. Charmon looked up and there he was, his bright orange reflecting the moonlight. She had been concentrating so hard on searching for a night spot that she had not realized the moon was out. Looking up into the night sky with the moon and the stars gazing back at her, she wondered if they too would benefit from the supernatural changes soon to come. Since the night lights were also parts of what the Lifegiver had designed, she assumed they would be included.

"Charmon, where are you? Come back to me," Narchom teased. She had that uncanny look on her face when she was absorbed in her innermost thoughts.

"I was just thinking how marvelous it is that the heavens are the works of the Lifegiver's hands. Isn't it beautiful?" she asked sleepily. When she yawned, he chuckled.

"Come let us get some rest." Peering into the space, he checked the cubbyhole first to make sure it was empty and safe for them. He allowed her to go in first and then he followed. They would need a fresh start for the day ahead. On this night Narchom did not need feel a to wrap himself in his flyers. Assuming since he had spent so much time today singing to the Lifegiver, Narchom figured there was no need to hear His voice anymore tonight.

Dawn woke them up. The first sliver of the morning light peeked into the cubbyhole. Somehow their eyes opened.

'How is it possible to be so refreshed after the previous day we just experienced?' they both thought.

Today was the day for them to meet with the Flutterbys. Now it was Narchom's turn to be impressed by his mate. Charmon's specialty was the ability to talk to many creatures at one time. Having a private moment with the Lifegiver is how she discovered her gift. Charmon had been sitting with her eyes closed, talking in her heart to the Lifegiver. Initially she did not realize what was happening until every creature she thought of came seeking her out. At first, she thought it was coincidence, or by chance. A specific incident undoubtedly convinced her that she attracts others to herself. She could still remember it as if it happened yesterday and thought of it often.

'I was out enjoying my morning. As I fluttered over a wee dirt mound, I looked down and I saw a Tan tribe. I was amazed by their tireless work. Watching them, the Lifegiver reminded me that the Tan's ways were wise; how they had no guide, overseer, or ruler but yet they provided their meat in the summer and gathered their food in the harvest. I responded in my heart to the Lifegiver that they

Honey Is Where The Heart Is

are so tiny, yet so strong. And they seem to carry the largest burdens on their backs as if they are not burdensome at all. I made my way to a nearby tree and rested on its smooth bark. Closing my eyes, I allowed my flyers to fall to my sides. Hearing the patter of little feet, I opened my eyes. Coming towards me up the trunk of the tree was a troop of the Tans. Intrigued by their actions, I remained in my place. Thinking they would simply march on by me, I sat motionless. To my surprise, they created a circle around me. I wondered what this unannounced encounter was about. Emerging from the circle, the largest one stepped forward and said to me,

"You have blessed us with your words. We are honored, you who can leave the ground, see us as strong despite our tiny size." I was puzzled! I was hesitant to ask but I had to. Was it possible? With my orange and black flyers towering over him, I braced myself for a response.

"Did you hear what I just said?"

"Yes, we all heard it here," he said pointing to his head, "and here," pointing to his heart.

Ever since that day, she allowed her gift to be used when it was needed. Hovering together in the cubbyhole, she sensed she needed his encouragement for the petition she was about to make. Since they believed that if the two of them touched and agreed on anything and asked the Lifegiver to do it for them, she and Narchom allowed their antennae to entangle. Today, Charmon would appeal to all the Flutterbys. It was time to declare to them the good news that restoration was coming to creation.

"Can I? Can I? Can I?" Noli insisted, bouncing and springing on all four paws around Ilon as she walked out into the dusk.

"What is he so excited about now?" Lino questioned Ilon. Turning towards her Mepaw, she responded,

"He wants to play in the tall grass today…alone…and I'm trying to decide…" Lino stopped her in mid-sentence.

"What happened to your shoulder?" she asked, noticing the

reddened scars on her golden frame.

"It's nothing. It's fine," she stated. Hoping to quickly change the subject, she asked, "So do you think we should let him go play by himself?"

"Can I? Can I? Can I?" he asked again, this time bouncing around Lino. On his last bounce, he lost his balance tumbled into the dirt. Both his maternal elders laughed. Ilon gingerly picked him up out of the dirt and brushed him off. Licking the side of his face she declared,

"You are my heritage from the Lifegiver. The fruit of my womb. You are my reward. Now go on, but just for a little while."

Noli squirmed his way out of her grasp. This time, he landed on all fours. Making his way towards the tall grass, he crouched low, almost on his belly. He learned this by watching and mimicking his elders. Turning to look back at his elders before he entered, he paused. He wanted to be sure they were both still watching him; he loved the attention. Entering it quickly, the curtain of grass closed behind him.

The scene within the grass looked different from the outside. Inside, Noli was big and strong. He had a crown of hair about his head and a thick powerful tail. Here he could forget that he was the young one. Creeping through his jungle, he pretended he was king. All the other creatures had to bow to him. Strutting about, he held his head high. Pretending the high grass was very tall trees, it did not matter that the grass was taller than him. As king his subjects were the creeping crawling things of the earth. The only problem Noli had not conquered yet was his roar. He was determined to voice his call. Gathering all the strength he could muster, he threw back his head, opened his mouth wide, and let it loose,

"Mew, mew, mew!" Still the same result, his roar had not changed. It was only louder this time. Losing his balance, he fell backwards. He lay there giggling, so happy that his elders let him play in the tall grass.

The lone pair of eyes continued to watch the innocent one through the grass. Gradually their color changed. The bright color of the morning sun in them gave way to the burning, red glare of temptation. The shadow held its breath so as not to be detected. Opening his mouth, his tongue dangled. He licked his lips and imagined what the young flesh would taste like. He stealthily moved

Honey Is Where The Heart Is

around to get behind the little one. He had a plan; stay down wind so as not to be detected.

'I will enjoy this one,' he thought to himself. Anpreth inhaled deeply, igniting the same sensation from their first encounter. He remembered his smell, the aroma of fear. He honestly did not know which he enjoyed more, the scent of fear or the taste of flesh. He stepped so lightly that it seemed his paws barely touched the ground. Impossible as it seemed, his goal was not to make any noise. Even though their kind was different, he knew their ears were as sharp as theirs. Being a little one did not matter; he might still sense him there. Just a few more steps and he would be upon him.

Oblivious to the intruder, Noli did not know he was being watched. In his innocent play, he was crouched on the ground giving orders to his subjects. As he laid there, he began to get comfortable. The little one in him getting sleepy overtook the mighty king he had been portraying. With his head nodding to one side, his eyes began to get heavy.

Anpreth was disappointed. He watched as drowsiness overtook the little one. If he was asleep, then there was no fear. Without fear, there was no excitement. And without the excitement, this would be an ordinary meal. Forgetting his plan for a moment Anpreth chuckled aloud,

"At least it's a good meal." No sooner than he let the words escape, he realized his error. Noli stirred, lifted his head, and looked around. Anpreth crouched low in the grass, regretting that he had spoken. Noli stood to his paws, ears straight up.

'I hear something,' the little one thought to himself, *'what is that?'* His curiosity getting the better of him, he walked deeper into the grass. He had played in the tall grass plenty of times, but this sound he had not heard before. It was a faint buzz.

Enhoy had decided to do something different today. She left the sanctity of the flowers and headed out on a different path. Flying farther than usual, she came upon a span of tall grass. Usually she did not bother with grass, but since she was experiencing the unordinary, she flew into it. The grass was tall, thin, and wispy Since it had no wide leaves to slow her down, maneuvering around was easy. She flew faster, buzzing through it, enjoying the wispy grass gliding over her wings.

Hearing something coming towards him in the grass, Noli stopped walking. He peered through it but could not see anything. Fear overtook him, and now he was afraid! Wanting to get out of the grass immediately, he turned towards the lair and ran as fast as he could, the grass smacking him in the face. Then, he felt something was on his tail! The buzzing was loud and clear and right behind him. He began to call out as he ran,

"Mepaw, Mepaw!"

Anpreth crouched low in the grass, departing from the area. He did not know what caused the little one to flee, but he knew it was time to leave. His yelping would bring the attention of his elders and he did not want to be here if they came. The desire to live outweighed the disappointment to feast on an innocent one. Slowly, walking back to his own lair that he shared with his brother, his sun-colored eyes adjusted to the oncoming dark. He left alone …and hungry.

Honey Is Where The Heart Is

CHAPTER EIGHTEEN

When the three of them entered the Throne Room, they all noticed that its brightness had significantly faded. The Queen, now completely pale, was seated on her throne. She appeared haggard, tired, and depleted. Barely able to move, she mustered enough strength to lift her head to greet them.

"Mother, what are you doing? You shouldn't be sitting up," Y'nohe lightly scolded as he walked towards her. Seeming to use all her strength, she smiled. She liked the fact that he addressed her as mother, something he did not often call her. He normally addressed her as his queen.

"Come to me, the three of you." Y'nohe and Nyohe quickly moved towards her. Hyeon hesitated. Nyohe, sensing her anxiety, stepped back towards her, took her by the hand, and motioned her to come too. Her sons stood on opposite sides of her and Hyeon in front of her.

"I want to speak to each of you before Lifegiver sends for me. The time is near." She reached forward and grasped Hyeon's hand, making her gasp. First the Queen pulled her close and hugged her tight. Then she motioned for her servant to kneel down before her. The Queen leaned forward and spoke,

"My dearest Hyeon, you are such a blessing to me. The time you have given to serve your Queen has been recorded by the Lifegiver. He knew who I needed, and He placed you at my side. I am so grateful! You were never my servant, but my daughter that I never had. I ask before I leave that you care for my family as you have cared for me." Never allowing the Queen to see her emotions, her composure vanished. Tears flowed from her eyes. She leaned forward and kissed her Queen. It warmed the Queen's heart and she hugged her back even tighter. Reluctantly unwrapping herself from Hyeon's grasp, she took the hand of her sons. Turning to Nyohe first she said,

"I leave you in good hands my child. Not only did I enjoy being your Queen, it was a blessing to me to have you as my own. Your joy is contagious and many times your laughter gave me strength when nothing else could. Now I have a confession. I am so jealous of you and your dreams!" The four of them laughed, their chuckles echoing off the walls. "You are one of a kind. Stay that way, the way the Lifegiver intended. Did He not say that He created those who are peculiar?" Again, they all laughed, but this time the Queen's laugh turned into a soft cough. Y'nohe rested his hand on her shoulder. Seeing the concern on all their faces, she assured them,

"I'm fine, I'm okay, now let me finish." Trying to spare every breath his mother had left, Y'nohe pleaded,

"My Queen, you don't have to say another word." Turning her focus on Y'nohe she demanded,

"No, I must speak, I must! She is on her way! And now I say to you, the Lifegiver bless you, and keep you. The Lifegiver makes His face shine upon you and be gracious to you. The Lifegiver lift up His countenance upon you and give you peace." With her last breath, she gasped, "Only she can light the way." And for the first time since Onyhe had been Queen, the glow in the Palace diminished. The colony came to a stop. They all knew their Queen was gone. No light meant no queen. Y'nohe, Nyohe, and Hyeon held tight to the Queen, faithfully believing that this darkness would give way to a new light.

Honey Is Where The Heart Is

He heard the flowing river before he saw it. He could smell the refreshing lure of the water. He exhaled from relief. Not only would he quench his thirst, but also immerse himself in it to cleanse away the many layers of grunge collected from his travels.

'Am I close to my destination?' he thought. Since his plan was to go to wherever he was being led, he had no clue. The need to repeatedly put one paw in front of the other subsided. His limbs finally gave their control back to him. Finally reaching the water's edge, he dunked his whole head in, shook it from side to side, and filled his mouth with the cool water. It was such a pleasure to imbibe in what had been missed. He had come to appreciate the rain and the storms. Without them, he would not be able to enjoy the moment. Knowing that drinking too much water could send his empty stomach into shock, he struggled to control the urge to fill his belly. Deciding to focus on his surroundings, he looked around. Across the river, not too far from where he stood, he noticed an area covered with tall, wispy weeds.

"That tall grass looks like a good place to get some rest." He took one more gulp and then headed out across the land. Reaching the edge of the field, he quickly entered. The grass closed behind him like a curtain.

Moving quickly for the opening to their lair, Ilon's muscles tensed as she bolted into the clearing where they all slept.

"Ilon, what is it?" her elder asked. Then Lino heard what caused Ilon to move so quickly. By the time the two female defenders reached the edge of the tall grass, the little one emerged, crying out in fright at the top of his lungs,

"Mepaw, Mepaw, Mepaw!"

They braced themselves for whatever would chase him from

the grass. After a few moments, they looked at one other, then at Noli, then at the tall grass. He was still hopping around, yelping for help. By this time, Inol emerged from the other side of the tall grass.

"Noli, Noli, what's wrong? Calm down!" he instructed as he picked up the little one, cradling him under his front legs. Squirming in his Grand One's arms, Noli stopped yelling long enough to say,

"Don't you hear it? Don't you hear it?" His three elders surrounded him.

"Hear what, Noli?" his Mepaw asked.

"It was following me, chasing me, buzz!" The three of them were confused. Inol lifted the little one higher in the air when he heard it, a muffled buzz. Sitting down, he placed Noli on his lap. He grabbed his little tail and fingered it to its tip. At the end of his tail, entangled in his delicate, sparse hair mixed with broken weeds was a wee passenger.

Because of her peculiar color, Inol did not believe his eyes. Using his huge paw, one claw, and with delicate precision, he untangled the hair from around her legs. Since the weeds had her wings bound, all she could do was buzz. The more debris he cleared away, the better he could recognize what it was. It was an Eeb.

Already afraid, she saw the huge paw coming towards her. Now terrified, Enhoy watched as the beast raised his claw. Then she remembered her dream. The enormous creature was freeing her from her bonds. In order to help him complete her freedom, she stopped struggling He even brushed away the dirt from her fuzzy body. Placing her in his huge paw, he held her up for the others to see.

"This was what the 'bzz bzz' was coming from!" All three elders leaned back and laughed. Noli, done with his yelping and hopping around, changed his cry to an inquiry,

"What is it? What is it? I wanna see!" Grand One lowered his paw so he could see what was in his hand. Noli reached out to touch her.

"Noli, no," Ilon said, and gently tapped his paw.

"What is it?" he asked again. Choking back emotion, Inol said,

"It is an Eeb." Turning to Enhoy he asked,

"Are you hurt?" Getting up and standing in his paw, she replied,

Honey Is Where The Heart Is

"No, I am fine." Surprising everyone, Inol asked,

"I know this is a lot to ask, but can you visit with us for a while? I just want to make sure you are okay, you know, well enough to fly back to where you live," he chuckled, "I don't expect that the tall grass is your usual place is it?"

"Well my wings are a little beat up from my unexpected ride. I can stay for a while." Noli and Ilon decided to keep her company while Inol and Lino entered the lair. As usual, Lino perceived that her mate's mind was preoccupied. Lino waited until they were deeper into their den then walked up behind him and asked,

"Inol, what is it?" Taking a moment to collect himself and trying to contain the lump in his throat, Inol opened his mouth to speak. The only thing that released was his tears that flowed down his face. He leaned against his mate and sobbed. Tears he had been holding for years gushed free. It took all of Lino's strength to support him. He let all the emotions escape he had been holding since that eventful day. Slowly he wrapped his legs around her and hugged her deeply. The tighter he squeezed, the less the tears flowed. Then he began to giggle. Unwrapping his arms from around her, Inol grinned at his mate. Neither surprised nor confused, Lino smiled back. She expected what he would say next.

"I can tell her!" he expressed, "I can finally tell her!" With the way he was dancing about, she wondered if she needed to calm him down. Deciding against that, she let him have his moment. Especially since this was the moment he had long waited for.

Honey Is Where The Heart Is

CHAPTER NINETEEN

Only the Flutterbys knew about this place they were destined for. Charmon led the way with Narchom following close behind her. He had never seen her move so quickly. The orange and black became a blur as they fluttered along. All the time she spent emitting and calling out to the others, he thought she would be exhausted. She was not. She was up, excited, and ready to go. She did not seem to remember how far she had to go but he did. He was tiring already. Finally able to catch his breath and get up beside her, he panted,

"Charmon, slow down; you will be tired by the time we get there!"

"No, I won't," she said, in between flutters, "they are seeking me out. I can hear them so clearly; that means I need to get there so they will know who called them." She did not miss one flutter. He knew it was futile to argue. She was fixated on her goal at hand. Nothing could keep her from her purpose.

They were headed for The Bloom. It existed for the Flutterbys. No one could describe it; having to be in order seen to be explained. Even the Lifegiver spoke of its beauty, saying, 'consider the flowers how they grow; they toil not, they spin not;

and yet I say that nothing in all its glory is arrayed like any of these.' Normally it took a day for them to get there, but at the speed that Charmon was moving, Narchom determined they could get there sooner. He was surprised yet relieved when he heard her say,

"Not too much farther now." For a Flutterby, fluttering faster than usual could be dangerous. Their flyers were delicate and not designed for speed. Instead they were intended for gliding and hovering. "This is it!" she exclaimed.

'Did she just speed up again?' Narchom questioned internally. But he understood why.

Approaching quickly was what the Flutterbys called the Fortress. It was a tall hedge, tightly packed with spiky thorns that protected The Bloom from other creatures. The Flutterbys simply flew up and over it. The two of them climbed higher and higher. A lifetime seemed to pass before they reached the top of the Fortress. They fluttered over the edge, the view taking their breath away. What a sight to see! For them, it was like looking onto a promised land! Every color imagined was present below them. Only the Lifegiver could have created such a masterpiece. Oranges, blues, and reds mingled with yellows, whites, and pinks. The secret of The Bloom was that every kind of flower that contained flower dust existed here. A sample of a white orchid, a deep orange lily, and a pink zinnia was found here. Yellow buttercups, purple violets, creamy honeysuckle, and brown and yellow sunflowers were there. Red geraniums, blue hydrangeas, red and black-centered poppies, and pale-yellow snapdragons were here. And not to forget the plentiful lilac colored milkweed. This place was a possible smorgasbord for the Flutterbys and any creature or creeping crawling thing that depended on the precious flower dust, it was paradise.

Many Flutterbys were scattered about in The Bloom. They all seemed to look up simultaneously to see Narchom and Charmon descending to them. The two of them rested on a sunflower; large enough to hold them both and tall enough for them to be seen by all. As fast as they were moving, Charmon thought Narchom would need a minute to rest, but as soon as his feet touched the flower's face, he spoke,

"Thank you, those of our kind for heeding the call. Today the Lifegiver brings you good news! It is time for the restoration of

Honey Is Where The Heart Is

creation! He is sending one who will take all that she is and make us anew. But the Lifegiver sent me here to encourage you all and to bless each of your tribes." The Flutterbys flapped their flyers in agreement. It was so many of them that it generated a slight breeze. The tops of the flowers swayed back and forth.

First, Narchom turned his attention to the Waltsaillow. Of the Flutterbys, they were the largest. Even though they were gentle. peaceful creatures, their appearance garnered an opposite effect. They had long weapon-like features on the ends of their rear flutters. Sometimes they liked the notion that other creatures thought they were warriors carrying weapons. But warriors did not spend their time replenishing the citrus trees. Lemons, oranges, and grapefruit were the only things they seemed to attack. To them he declared,

"The Lifegiver knows your works, charity service, and faith. He knows your patience. You are considered last but will be more than the first. But He has one charge to bring to your attention. You have one among you who misuses the fruit of her labors; yet you have not brought her to justice. He gave her space to change her ways, of misusing the gift given to her, but she has not. He will deal with her Him- self so as not to put the burden on you. And you of the Waltsaillows He says to hold fast until the restoration comes, and He will allow you to see the glory of the morning!" Narchom did not pause to give them time to react. Next, he focused his attention to the Yorcive. With his back to the Waltsaillows, he could not see that they fluttered about in excitement, creating a cloud of color in the air. To the Yorcives he decreed,

"The Lifegiver knows your works, and you have a name that thrives. Be watchful and strengthen the things which remain after the change comes. Though you pretend to be as others, you have not defiled what I have given you. You are worthy of your works!" For the Yorcives, this was uplifting news to hear. Because they too were orange and black, they were often mistaken for those of the Romchan tribe, like Narchom and Charmon. Instead of revealing who they really were, they let other creatures believe they could hear from the Lifegiver too. But on this day, they were grateful that the Lifegiver cared for them anyway.

The Larimda awaited their turn. This tribe of the Flutterbys struggled with their appearance. In their creeping crawling state before they are given their flyers, there are spikes all over them. When motionless, they resemble dead leaves. In spite of how they looked, they've contributed much life to creation. But Narchom's news would change how they felt about themselves. To them he admonished,

"The Lifegiver knows your works. Before you He has placed an open opportunity, and no one can keep it from you. For though you have little confidence, you deemed His gift to you as precious and did not deny that He blessed you. Once creation has been restored, you will feel no condemnation about your appearance. Be patient and you will understand why He made you as you are!" Narchom thought to himself,

'How could such lovely creatures be mistaken for something dead?'

Their excitement caused waves of flutters from all who were there. Narchom paused to let them collect themselves. He waited until the breeze from all the fluttering subsided. The Kippers tribe knew it was their turn next. Even though they were Flutterby, they darted around very quickly. As Narchom blessed the others, they had been trying the entire time to sit still. Their short, stocky bodies, large eyes, and crochet-hooked antennae contrasted their unusual capacity of speed. To them he encouraged,

"The Lifegiver knows your works, that some of your tribe is either not using your gift as best as you can, or not using it at all. But He says that during the restoration, He will speak to you directly. And He wants you to get closer to Him and let Him refine you. Because He loves you, He chastens you. Be excited about the change that the restoration shall bring unto your tribe." That was the inspiration they needed to hear. The leaders had been encouraging their tribe to focus more on the Lifegiver. When the Kippers realized that the Lifegiver loved them anyway, no matter their shortcomings, that sent them into frenzy. They moved so quickly that they resembled a Ghimmundrib tribe flying about.

The only tribe left was the Romchan, who Narchom and Charmon belonged to. They were the ones who stayed in constant contact with Him on behalf of creation. They were here to support the other Flutterbys and did not expect the Lifegiver to have something specific for them. To their surprise, Narchom turned to them and stated,

Honey Is Where The Heart Is

"What is the declaration that you've heard many times, 'the days are prolonged and every vision fails'? Today the Lifegiver says to you, our tribe, to me, my mate that He will make this saying to cease, and it shall no more be used as wisdom. He says the days are at hand for the effect of every vision we've imagined. For He is the Lifegiver. When He speaks, what He speaks shall come to pass. The words He gives us shall be prolonged no more. Continue to call unto Him and He will answer you and show you great and mighty things that you don't know!"

Turning to Charmon, Narchom embraced her. Everything the two of them were tasked to do was completed. The Romchans fluttered about elated to hear the Lifegiver's decree. The Flutterbys remained in The Bloom for the rest of the day. Knowing they needed to leave, none of them wanted to. But they had to return home to share all that the Lifegiver told them with the rest of creation.

Still engulfed in darkness, the Eebs prepared their Queen for her final place in the colony. Hyeon was given the honor of preparing her body. Hyeon did not think she was worthy of the task, but Y'nohe encouraged her that his mother would have wanted her to be the one to perform it. She had two of the Queen's servants with her to assist her. Since the light of the Queen was out, the Eebs responsible for keeping the Palace in good working order created small openings in strategic places to let in some light. It was still dreary and dark, but they managed. Hyeon was able to see just enough to do what needed to be done. The Queen was placed on a special pedestal. She carefully folded the Queen's wings around her colorless body. Gingerly, she wrapped her in the specially prepared sage leaves. The leaves had been collected by the two servants, making sure to preserve their fragrance. They had them soaked in honey and then dried. The servants sprinkled her body with flower dust; from every kind of flower that the Queen had personally visited. Doing this honored the Queen and the many flowers to which she helped give life. After her body was completely wrapped,

Hyeon sent the servants to inform the King that the Queen was prepared for the procession through the Palace. Left there alone with the Queen, Hyeon could not hold the tears any longer. She flung herself across the Queen's body and sobbed.

"I am going to miss you so much! You were kind and gentle to me. I never felt like your servant. I felt like your own. I regret not letting you treat me as such. I was so worried about not pleasing the Lifegiver the right way that I missed receiving all the love you had for me. I realized too late that He put me here with you so you could love me, as you saw I needed. I am so sorry! Please forgive me!" Her intimate moment was interrupted.

"No need to cry, Hyeon. She knew how much you loved her." She quickly stood up, wiped her faced and turned to see Nyohe standing there. He gazed at her with such care on his face.

"Come, let's go and allow the servants to bring the Queen out for all of us to love before we take her to her resting place." He stretched out his hand for hers and she reluctantly received it. He smiled at her.

Two of the sentinels, towering over them all, picked up the Queen on her pedestal and began the trek through the Palace. They walked every corridor with Y'nohe, Nyohe, and Hyeon following behind them. As they passed through, many Eebs who loved their Queen, lined the way. They garnished the floor with flower petals and waved their wings as her body went by. Some even wept. They would deeply miss her. Finally, they reached the special chamber that had been prepared for her. It was so new that the waxy substance was still warm. The two sentinels placed her in her tomb and moved out of the way for the two servants to cover the opening. They moved quickly, covering the entrance, patting and smoothing the wax as they worked. Y'nohe stepped forward. He struggled with what he would say for this moment, but he believed if he opened his mouth, the Lifegiver would give him the right words to say. He turned to face the multitude of Eebs waiting for his encouragement.

The king said, "Today our Queen leaves us, but don't be dismayed. She spoke of this day and gave us hope that the new queen is on her way. Her love for us will not be forgotten. The way she served all of us will be remembered. Let us all look to this day not as the day she left us, but as the day that she moved us forward. Remember, precious in the sight of the Lifegiver is the death of one

Honey Is Where The Heart Is

of His beloved creations."

They all bowed simultaneously, even Y'nohe and Nyohe. Y'nohe took the special container with their initial batch of honey preserved in it, turned it on its golden end, and made an imprint with it in the softened wax. Now, that it had been marked, everyone would recognize her chamber.

CHAPTER TWENTY

Enhoy ended up staying with the Onlis longer than she expected. Her wee body exhausted more than she realized. By the time she left them, she was well rested. She said goodbye to everyone, especially Noli, and headed on her way. This time she decided to fly over the grass instead of through it. Inol watched as she flew away. His heart was lighter, and his mind was clear. He did not waste a minute. Turning his attention to his offspring, he asked her,

"Ilon, can we talk?"

"Of course, Mepaw. What about?"

"Come Noli, let's give them some time by themselves," Lino said, leading him out of the lair.

"Can we go play in the tall grass, Mepaw?" he asked, already getting excited. She laughed.

"Haven't you had enough of the grass for once today? Okay, come on but only for a little while," and they left the other two alone.

Inol did not know where to start. Sitting down on his haunches, he motioned for Ilon to join him. They had not had an intimate conversation in a while. She purposely sat close to him, but instead of her haunches, she lay on her stomach with her legs nestled under her.

"Ilon, can you tell me something?"

"What's that Mepaw?" He loved it when she called him that.

"Tell me why you are so angry with the Lifegiver." Her demeanor changed. She shifted her paws and turned her head. She clawed the dirt. Even though she did not answer immediately, he did not question her again. She took a deep breath and cleared her throat. Knowing this moment was inevitable, she had to answer him so her heart could be completely healed.

Finally, she spoke, "He took my family from me. I imagined he and I would be together forever. And is it fair that Noli only has one elder? He would have added to us, yet he was taken away from us! How do you think I feel watching you and Mepaw sharing your love for one another? I missed that chance. How many cold nights have I tried to stay warm by myself or wanted to lean on someone like Mepaw leans on you? I have been so alone. My comforter was taken from me, yet I am sup- posed to be glad about this? How much more does the Lifegiver expect me to bear? And what about my little one? He doesn't have time with his elder because he isn't here. He was supposed to help me shape and form who Noli was to be, but he's not here. And what if Noli wasn't supposed to be my only one? So many things were taken from me, not just him," she barely whispered it all out. Then her dam of tears burst. Inol held back his tears, believing this moment in time was so perfect. Now he could witness the Lifegiver to showing her how much He really loved her. Inol decided he had to let her talk it all out first.

"Ilon, you are so loved and don't realize it. The day I returned without your mate and I told you he was killed in the hunt, that wasn't what happened." She stopped crying for a moment. Wiping her tears away with the back of her paw, she asked,

"What, what do you mean?"

"Your mate had to make a choice," he paused, "your life or his." Not understanding what he meant, in between her sniffles, she asked again,

"What do you mean?"

"No one really understands the actions of the Lifegiver. His ways are higher than our ways and His thoughts are higher than our

Honey Is Where The Heart Is

thoughts. All He expects us to do is trust Him. When your mate approached the Lifegiver and asked Him to spare your life, he told Him he would take your place." Sitting upright on her haunches, she asked,

"Why would he do that? I don't understand." He knew he would have to tell her the entire matter.

"When you were born, the Lifegiver came to us and told us He had blessed us with your life because He needed you. He told us He would need your life when you were older for a specific purpose as a sacrifice. Because we trusted the Lifegiver we raised you as He asked us to. We loved you with all our hearts because we believed we wouldn't have you forever and decided not to tell others, until we met your mate. We knew it wasn't fair to not tell him what the Lifegiver shared, so we told him. Still, he desired to be your mate and decided he would love you with all his heart until the Lifegiver called for you." Ilon was speechless. She had no idea that these things had happened in her life. Focusing on her elder, she continued to listen.

"He came to me in the middle of the night and shared that he went to the Lifegiver and vowed to Him he would die for you. Because he loved you so much, he would be the sacrifice in your place. He made me promise to tell you that he was killed in the hunt because he didn't want you to hate the Lifegiver for taking his life. But that didn't work!" They both laughed, Ilon nervously.

He continued, "He asked me if I would go with him on the day the Lifegiver called for him so there could be a witness to his love for you. Of course I didn't want to go, but I knew one day, I would have to tell you. So, when the Lifegiver called for him, we headed out to where the Lifegiver sent us. At first it was odd to us. He told us to wait in a vineyard."

"As we waited there, He began to tell us how much He loved His two-leg children, but they needed to be taught to trust Him. He said they continued to do evil in His sight and they did that which was right in their own eyes. Because of this, He had to send one to deliver them out of the hands of the two-leg Philistines. He told your mate that He needed to use him to show the one named Samson how to yield to His Spirit. We were to wait in this vineyard until Samson came by with his elders. He said we would recognize him because his hair would be long and thick, almost like ours. And we waited. When we heard them coming along the path, your mate jumped out of the vineyard at the one named Samson. I didn't know what had come over your mate. I could only trust that he had listened to the direction of the Lifegiver. Your mate roared against him. The Spirit of the Lifegiver came mightily upon the one named Samson, and he rent your mate as if he were a young one. And without a weapon in his hand. I wanted to help, to roar against him too, but I knew that this was the plan of the Lifegiver. My heart was torn. Even though his life was taken, I got to witness the Spirit of the Lifegiver fall upon this two-leg one." He paused as he remembered what he saw that day. As hard as he tried, he could not put into words what he had witnessed.

Ilon registered a mixture of emotions. She was no longer angry with the Lifegiver for now she understood certain things that happened in her life. How her mate treated her as if he would never let her out of his sight. How her elders had showered her with such love, more than the others in their tribe. Why she had mistakenly loathed the Lifegiver; and right now, the compassion for her Mepaw. He had been concealing everything all this time. How painful and hard it must have been for him as she disrespected him and walked rebelliously for so long. She rushed to his side and embraced him. He was so caught off guard that he almost fell over.

"I love you so much Mepaw. I love you so much!" It was at that moment that Noli sauntered in covered with weeds, followed by his Mepaw. Lino stopped at the entrance to watch her tribe back together, in love again. She thought about what the Lifegiver had shared with her when this all began.

'And now abide faith, hope, and love, these three. But the greatest of these is love.'

Noli strolled over to his Grand One and Mepaw. He snuggled his way in between the two of them. He always took advantage of receiving love. The elders surrounding him laughed. Continuing his story, Inol said to Ilon,

"But you know something? The Lifegiver left a reminder for us. Would you like to see it?" Ilon wrinkled her brow,

"A reminder? You mean like a marker?"

"Yes, to remind us that no greater love a mate has than to lay down his life for his mate. And it's beautiful! How about we take a

Honey Is Where The Heart Is

walk tomorrow just to see it?"

Honey Is Where The Heart Is

CHAPTER TWENTY-ONE

Still in awe from her previous encounter, Enhoy's plan was to return to her flower friends, spend some time with them, and share her unbelievable experiences of the day. She also wanted to replenish herself on their sweet nectar. Almost across the span of the tall grass, she noticed up ahead a group of Lyfs hovering.

'They are making a lot of noise,' she thought but continued on her way. Getting closer to them, she realized too late it was not the Lyfs, but something else. She gasped when she saw the creatures. Her friends, the Romchans, had not mentioned these creatures. They were black and white like her and even larger than the Spaws. Their heads were huge and their weapons at the end of their bodies even larger. Now worried, she thought,

'Did they see me?' Hoping she had not been noticed, she spun around and sped off in the other direction. One of the creatures, a Noreth, did see her. Turning to the mob, he urged on the others of his kind,

"Look! Is that an Eeb? Let's have a meal of this one!" He darted off after her with the others following. Flying with all her might, Enhoy was thankful that she had rested before leaving the Onlis. There were no flowers in sight for her to hide in. Glancing over her shoulder, she saw them headed for her.

"What do I do now?" She panicked. Fear was overtaking her. If terror consumed her, her wings would constrict. Knowing she would plummet to the ground to her doom, she commanded her wings to speed her along. In a moment of courage, she decided to do something she had never done before. Deep from her heart, she sent out an Eeb distress call. Enhoy cried out for help, hoping any colony of Eebs would hear her.

Y'nohe was sitting in the Throne Room on what was now his throne. He was attempting to get accustomed to sitting there. From this platform, he would now address the subjects of his Kingdom. Laughing to himself, he whispered,

"My subjects. My Kingdom." The sentinel rushed in, interrupting his thoughts

"My Lord please come quickly. We are receiving a distress call from an unknown Eeb!"

"A distress call?" Y'nohe jumped to his feet.

"Yes, my Lord, we need to know what you would have us to do!" The two of them immediately took flight, maneuvering their way through the twisting and turning of the tunnels inside the colony. Even though it was still dark they knew the way. All the sentinels and warriors had already assembled at the entrance, anticipating and preparing for battle. Now amongst his soldiers, Y'nohe removed his own weapon, placed it in his hand, and stood with his guards.

"My Lord, shall we send a return call?"

"Yes, an Eeb is an Eeb, one of our kind. If they need help, we must come to their aid. My warriors, prepare for attack!" The sentinels were the first line of their defense. They hovered at a distance from the colony, placing themselves as a shield before it. The other mighty warriors posted behind them. Y'nohe positioned at the entrance ready to defend his Eebs with his life. He began to send a return call for the distress one they received. Closing his eyes, he lifted his wings, and concentrated.

"We are here. Come to us. You are welcome here if you need safety." His wings began to vibrate, mustering all his strength to do so. Picking up the signal, he could feel himself guiding this Eeb to

Honey Is Where The Heart Is

them, to him. He continued to home in on the vibrations.

"My warriors, she is not too far now! Be ready!" he instructed. *'How did I know it was a female?'*

In disbelief, Enhoy was relieved. A colony had returned her distress call. It was a clarion to her soul, empowering her to fly faster and stronger. The horde was almost upon her. Their wings were so many and so loud! The din was deafening! With her life at stake, she refused to look back again. The Noreth in the lead shouted to those behind him,

"We almost have this Eeb! Don't give up!"

Much to her relief, she saw the colony that communicated with her. Up ahead she saw a line of the biggest Eebs she had ever seen; almost as large as the beasts chasing her. But what really caught her attention was the colony behind them. Enhoy had never seen anything so amazing! Surrounded by white columns, the colony was transfixed to the top of an arch. The Eebs opened ranks just enough for her to fly through. Seemingly the Noreth behind her was so close that he could have reached out and grabbed her wing. She was safe for now behind the wall of Eebs. The battle that ensued was unbelievable! She hovered there for a moment and watched, not sure where to go.

'Are they really fighting like this for me? But they don't know me.' she thought. Experiencing the call again, she turned towards the source of the signal. He was standing there at the entrance, so tall and regal with his wings up in the air, coaxing her.

'Is he the King?' she thought, *'but don't colonies only have Queens?'* Making her way over to him, she landed on the entrance platform. Not expecting her appearance, Y'nohe was speechless. Standing before him was an Eeb with white stripes where her yellow ones were supposed to be.

"Thank you, thank you for letting me come here. I didn't know what else to do," and she bowed before him. Lowering his wings and taking her by the shoulders, he lifted her up to stand before him. He responded with such confidence,

"No, you won't have to bow before anyone in this place." Y'nohe was concentrating so hard on the one before him that he forgot they were in the middle of a battle.

"My Lord, look out!" The Noreth that initially scouted

Enhoy had broken through the line and was heading towards them.

"I saw her first, so she's mine!" he bellowed and swung his weapon at them.

Y'nohe remained on that platform and fought with every tactic he had been taught. Even though this Noreth was larger than him, he did not waver and protected his domain. Pushing Enhoy to safety inside the entrance, he fought for her and his Eebs. Their weapons clashed and clanged against one another, both fighting for what they believed was theirs. But Y'nohe was the victor. Wielding his weapon with precision, he cut off the beast's wing, and then cut off its head. The beheaded form fell to the platform. Y'nohe kicked it, letting it fall to the ground with the bodies of the others. The Noreths gave up. Concluding they could not win, they resorted not to lose any more of their horde. They surrendered to their defeat, and sentinels chased the rest of them away. Never such a battle had been fought in this place!

It took some time for the colony to settle down. They were all abuzz about the battle and wondered about the female Eeb that had arrived in the chaos. They all noticed her unique appearance, but it did not matter to any of them. Because their King had accepted her, they all trusted him and followed his lead. Y'nohe had asked Hyeon to escort Enhoy to an inner chamber so that she could sit for a moment and collect her composure. Once inside the chamber, Hyeon shared,

"I've never seen our King fight that way." Enhoy agreed,

"He was impressive, wasn't he?" She watched as Hyeon moved about, doing everything she could to make her comfortable. Breaking the silence, Enhoy asked, "What is your name? I am Enhoy." Hyeon paused. It was the same question asked of her by their previous Queen and their newly crowned King. Bowing elegantly before her, she boldly replied without hesitation,

"My name is Hyeon, and I am here for whatever you need."

"Thank you." They smiled at each other.

Y'nohe returned to the Throne Room. So perplexed by the moment, he did not know what to do. He sent one of the servants to summon Nyohe. Pacing back and forth, he waited for his brother to arrive. Finally, Nyohe walked through the door.

"What took you so long? I need you!" Ynohe exclaimed raising his voice and throwing his arms up in the air.

Honey Is Where The Heart Is

"My brother, I mean, my Lord, how can I help you?" Nyohe responded jokingly.

"This isn't the time to joke around. I believe our new Queen is here!" Y'nohe stopped walking and stood there with his hands on his sides.

"What do you mean 'here'? You mean in the colony?" he asked, pointing towards the floor. Becoming more serious, Nyohe's attitude changed,

"Yes. You know the distress call we got today? The one that initiated the battle?"

"Yes."

"The distress call echoed from one that was black and white. And it was I who responded to her from me, I mean, from us. I believe it's her, our Queen." Y'nohe started pacing again. His younger brother stared at him with a puzzled look on his face.

"Why are you looking at me that way?" Y'nohe stopped moving and placed his hands on his sides. Thinking for a moment before he spoke, Nyohe responded,

"What's wrong?"

"What do you mean 'what's wrong'? Y'nohe retorted. Walking back and forth across the floor of the Throne Room, he admitted, "I don't know what to do!" In spite of the situation, Nyohe erupted with laughter. Here was his brother, the King, who had all the answers in his heart, yet feared he was clueless

"I see nothing funny about this. I ask for your help, and you laugh at me."

"I'm laughing at you because you keep forgetting who you are," he lovingly explained, "You are our King and the Lifegiver is for you, not against you. He has given you wisdom, knowledge, and revelation and you are not using it! Look at all He has shown you! Look at all he has revealed to you! Stop thinking you need to ask for the answers when you already have them!"

This time when Y'nohe paused his pacing, he stopped long enough for his racing mind to slow down. In his moment of peace, he realized the younger one was right. Having all the answers in his heart to guide him, he would just follow it. He crossed his arms and peered at Nyohe.

"Are you sure you are not the one to be King?" he asked,

laughing at himself.

"Yes, I am sure. Now I will let Hyeon know you are ready for her. What's her name?" Y'nohe looked puzzled. "You didn't ask her name?" Nyohe inquired, laughing as he left the throne room, "you do need my help, and then some."

"You sent for me?" Enhoy asked. Attempting to compose herself, Enhoy nervously watched from the hallway. Hyeon had shown her the way and then left her at the door. Positioned behind his throne, Y'nohe turned and faced her. He remained there with his hands clasped behind his back.

"Yes, I did. Please come in." She entered the Throne Room, only taking two or three steps. The silence was awkward. Collecting himself and then clearing his throat, he spoke, "I'm sorry. In all that has happened today, I forgot to ask your name. I am Y'nohe. What is your name?"

"My name is Enhoy." Again, total silence. She stared at her tiny feet. Usually when she was nervous, her antennae would droop. Luckily for now, she was able to keep them upright.

"Well Enhoy what a day we've had. It was an honor to defend you today. For your safety, I am glad you sent that distress call." Thankful that she was looking down at her feet, he tried hard not to stare but he failed. Hyeon performed an excellent job on her fuzzy form. Her black was deep as night and her bright white reminded him of something he had seen before. Unable to recall what it was, he refocused on her. He could not help but to notice her well-polished wings and her body that glistened with dew oil. Taking a step towards him, she confessed,

"I could hear you calling to me, loud and clear, and that has never happened to me before." Somewhat puzzled and surprised, he asked,

"You've never called to another Eeb before?" Moving towards him again, she answered,

"No, I've been alone for a long time." Y'nohe stepped out from behind the throne and leaned against it. His gaze intensified, making her self-conscious.

"Why have you been alone?" he asked.

"I was part of a colony. Then one day my Queen made me leave them. I don't know why. I miss them so much." She lowered her head to hide the forming tears. Seizing the opportunity to explain

Honey Is Where The Heart Is

her presence, Y'nohe did not hesitate. Almost whispering the words, he said,

"I believe you belong here with us...with me." He waited for her reaction. Compelled to look at him, she raised her head.

"Why do you believe that?" She forced herself to close her mouth, but amazement kept prying it open.

"We've dreamed you. We've envisioned your coming. We've all been waiting for you. I've been waiting for you; for you to be our Queen, and my Queen." He released all the words that had been burning in his heart since she had stepped into the room.

"Queen? A Queen? I am no one's Queen," she whispered defensively.

"I believe the Lifegiver sent you to us. In His infinite wisdom and love for His creation, He led you this way. And I can prove it to you."

"How are you able to prove to me, me a nobody, that I am your Queen?" He gestured for her to come to him. With her feet barely moving, she closed the distance between them.

"All you have to do is sit on the throne." Y'nohe was following his heart. He was hearing the instructions step by step.

"Sit on the throne? I can't ...," she tried to argue, but he interrupted her. stepped closer to her, looked into her eyes, and entreated softly,

"You asked me to prove it to you, then trust me." His eyes were so full of faith that it erased her doubts. His belief helped her unbelief. She was so at ease. Without saying another word, Enhoy stepped onto the platform of the Throne. She slowly turned, putting her back to the great chair, and sat down. As soon as her body filled the space, something happened.

Her whole body trembled. Closing her eyes, the unexplainable sensation filtered through her. Her white stripes began to glow and ebb. Flower dust from every kind of plant she had ever visited emanated from her body. The Throne was extracting it. Holding onto the arms of the chair for support, the glow and ebb became brighter and stronger. The honey in the colony began to glow. It began to swirl and change. It changed from its golden, amber color to a clear, champagne-tinged hue. And it was so bright, brighter than the Palace had ever been before. The light from it flowed through the entire colony! The light had returned! Enhoy could not move. She let the Throne do its work. It was sending a healing restoration through the colony. It was so powerful that it seeped through the holes that had been made to let in light. It flowed outside where creation was waiting. Every tree could feel it; every herb and plant could feel it; every animal and creature could feel it and every creeping and crawling thing could feel it. This was the beginning of the restoration of creation that had been foretold.

In his stupor, Y'nohe could only watch; he was dumbfounded, his eyes and mouth wide. It is one thing to hear the Lifegiver reveal a thing, but to believe it and witness it come to pass is another. Remembering what her white colored bands reminded him of, he walked over to the special cubby. He opened it and gracefully extracted the special container that held their first batch of honey. It was white as her bands; one end golden and the other, a pointed tip.

Finally opening her eyes, Enhoy sat there exhausted. She was too weak to move. Y'nohe circled the Throne to face her. Bowing before her, he set the container in her lap.

"This is for you my Queen." She was amazed that the object she dreamed was in her lap! It was curved, beautifully polished white, and had a pointed end. Recalling from her dream, the One had physically placed it on her chest. Just like she had dreamed, she picked up the object and hugged it close to her but this time, she began to cry. Her tears, not of sadness, but from relief. Enhoy was in the right place at the right time. She found home. Y'nohe asked,

"Is this enough proof, my Queen?" Still clutching the keepsake to her bosom, she lovingly reached out and touched Y'nohe's face,

"Yes, my King, this is enough."

Honey Is Where The Heart Is

CHAPTER TWENTY-TWO

The Onlis headed out for their walk. Noli led the way, taking directions from his Grand One. The two females lagged behind, taking their time to just enjoy the day.

"We are almost there," Inol turned, talking over his shoulder. For the fiftieth time, Noli asked again,

"What is it gonna be? And are we there yet?" Ilon scolded him,

"Noli, leave Grand One alone. He said we are almost there!" Lino laughed. She shared with Ilon that she had been the same way, many questions and always full of energy! She reminded her about the many nights she kept her Mepaw awake, wanting to either talk or play. They both laughed. As they followed Inol, Lino asked him,

"Do you think the vineyard is still there?" He shrugged in response. Surprised by her question, Ilon asked,

"Mepaw, you knew about this?"

"Of course I did. I was a comfort for your elder when he returned. And we have been talking to the Lifegiver together about it for all this time. We have learned to be strong for each other." Affectionately, Ilon bumped her mother with her hip, "and I love you too," her elder responded.

As planned, the four located the vineyard. Walking through it, they noticed the leaves were crisp, green and had a plush appearance. The ground soil was deep, dark, and moist. And the clusters of the fruit were enormous and full. Inol softly said,

"The last time I was here, this place was dry and barren. It is fertile now." Moving further into the vineyard, he spotted it; the marker he told them about. To get a better view, they all stepped out of the vineyard. Off to the side, nestled in its own safe place, was the carcass of an Onli. The weather cleansed bones glistened white and gleamed in the sun. Still connected, the shoulder and front leg bones looked like columns, and its backbone created an arch. And there, hanging in its ribcage was a colony of Eebs. Everyone was speechless, except for Noli who exclaimed with his usual excitement,

"Look Mepaw. Honey! And look, honey is where the heart is!"

Even in his death, her mate still expressed how much he loved her. The young innocent one was right. She imagined him there looking at her, and where the colony had positioned itself, beat his heart. All the love he had stored up for her was portrayed by the tangible sweetness that flowed through that place. Inol cuddled up beside his offspring,

"Ilon, you okay?" Mimicking her own offspring, she excitingly responded,

"Yes, my Grand One, thank you for bringing me here. I needed to see this."

"Well let's go, we don't want to disturb the Eebs. You know they are known for protecting their kind." In agreement with Lino's wisdom, everyone headed back. Looking up at his elder Noli innocently asked Ilon,

"Mepaw what was that we went to see?" Ilon responded,

"I will tell you when you are older okay?"

"Okay," he agreed. After contemplating his next adventure, he said, "I have an idea." Bracing herself for what he may possibly say and still amazed by his earlier comment, she asked,

"What's that?"

"Can we play in the tall grass tonight? I want to show you that I am not afraid!" He crouched low, skimming the ground,

Honey Is Where The Heart Is

pretending he was about to attack. She laughed.

"Okay, we'll go tonight but not for too long, okay?"

"Mepaw, mepaw!" Noli was pouncing on his elder, attempting to wake her up.

She forced her eyes open. He was reenergized and wide awake. Yawning, she asked him,

"What is it now Noli?"

"You said we could play in the tall grass tonight. See, the moon is out!" She had forgotten about the promise from earlier in the day.

"Okay we will go, but not too far and not too long." With the insistence of the younger Onli, she rose to her paws. They walked out of the lair, heading towards the tall grass. Lino called after them,

"The two of you be careful. There is a full moon tonight!"

"We will," Ilon responded and disappeared into the grass, the curtain of weeds closing behind them. Enjoying the cool night air, she watched Noli enjoy himself chasing the shadows. She realized they had walked a good distance from the lair, and decided it was far enough. Suddenly remembering where she was, she quickly grabbed Noli and said,

"Come on little one, time to go." But it was too late. She smelled him first, and then she saw the shadow. Ilon placed Noli behind her. She felt his young claws penetrate her skin. Speaking directly to the yellow, glowing eyes, she asked,

"What are you doing here?"

"I should ask you the same. Are you thinking about us?" Napreth taunted, his long tail whipping back and forth behind him.

"No, I'm not. I don't have a reason to. I am not one of 'you'," she answered, spitting the word back at him.

"Oh, so you are not one of us?" Another shadow appeared. Noli dug his claws deeper into his Mepaw's rear leg. He had seen these creatures before but initially, it was only one of them. Refusing to let fear consume her, Ilon knew if they smelled Noli's fear and hers, they would fight her even more. But she was prepared to die for her offspring. Her mate had given his life for hers, so she was ready to sacrifice her life for their young one. Even if she called for help, the others would not get to her in time to help. Knowing what she must do, she turned her head for a moment to speak to Noli.

"How dare she turn her back on us," Anpreth growled between clinched teeth. His eyes turned from their bright yellow to a coal-burning red; not from temptation for the innocent one, but from anger. Ilon ignored him.

"Noli," she whispered, "when I tell you to run, I want you to run get Grand One and Mepaw okay?" He nodded as she pried his tiny claws from her leg, "but you wait until I say 'run' okay?" Again, he nodded. She turned to face her aggressors, crouching low to attack. She charged the two shadows, catching them off guard,

"Run, Noli, run!" she growled. The little one took off, scampering through the tall grass. Noli ran the fastest he had ever run in his young life. Ilon contended for his life. Every time one of the brothers tried to escape from the clearing to pursue him, she would grab them with her claws, drawing them back into the fierce battle. Blood and hair, golden and deep night, was scattered everywhere. Piercing teeth and razor claws left their mark each time. Ilon defended herself against them as long as she could. With her strength leaving her, Napreth grabbed her rear leg, and pulled her to the ground.

"Grand One, Grand One!" Instead of his usual yelps, Noli was screaming this time. Inol and Lino instantly emerged from the entrance. They noticed the little one had returned alone. Seeing that his countenance was bathed in fear, Inol took off into the tall grass. Lino scooped up Noli and comforted him, hoping her family would survive the night.

'What is that noise?' he wondered. Earlier in the day, he had bathed and then wandered deep into the tall grass. Rested and clean, he had fallen asleep. The commotion awakened him from his sleep. Hearing loud yelps, he determined it was from an Onli in distress, so he quickly headed towards the sounds.

Anpreth joined his brother, standing over the battle bruised Ilon. Laughing menacingly Napreth asked,

"Now don't you wish you were one of 'them' now!" Ilon screamed at the top of her lungs,

Honey Is Where The Heart Is

"Never! I am proud to be an Onli!". Just as Napreth raised his paw to slash her face, something charged out of the tall grass, knocking them both over. It emitted such a roar. In her weakened state, Ilon thought

'I've heard him before.'

Another fight ensued. The Onli that charged from the tall grass was a stranger, unknown to her. As he fought, he moved with such agility and skill. Just in time, Inol stormed into the clearing. Letting out a mighty roar, he aided Ilon and pulled her safely to the edge of the tall grass. He turned to assist the stranger in the defense, but something unseen prevented him.

The Spirit of the Lifegiver came mightily upon this unnamed one. He rent Anpreth as if he were a young one. Even in her battered state, Ilon experienced the presence of the Lifegiver in this place and it was His presence that triggered her memory. Recalling the dream, the roar, and the ropes, she exclaimed in excitement,

"I am being rescued!" After disposing of Anpreth, the unnamed one turned his attention to Napreth. Cowering in fear and in awe of the one who now stood over him, Napreth braced himself. He knew this was the end of his life. Instead the unnamed one showed him mercy.

"Go!" he growled, "go and come here no more, or next time, I won't spare your life!" In shame, Napreth crawled to the edge of the tall grass, just as he had done before her elders. Reaching the edge of his escape, he fled off into the night.

The one without a name approached Inol and Ilon. Not one scratch did he have on him. His eyes were golden and piercing. He was majestic and mysterious, but something was quite different about him. Concentrating on his appearance, they concluded what it was; his hair about his head, full and billowy, was the same color as his body and his eyes! He was the same color all over, even his claws were golden. Questioning Inol he asked softly,

"Is she okay?"

"Yes, yes, she's a little beat up, but she is okay." Riveted, Inol stared at this stranger. He could not fathom that he again witnessed the Spirit of the Lifegiver but this time, upon one of his kind, "thank you for saving my Ilon's life." Looking down at Ilon, the unnamed one smiled deeply and responded,

"The pleasure was mine."

"You are a fine specimen of an Onli," Inol stated. "What is your name?"

"I am called Olin. I have traveled far and wide, allowing the Lifegiver to order my steps to the place He has prepared for me." Grinning, Inol offered him an invitation.

"You are welcome to rest here with us until He tells you to move on."

Ilon was speechless. After seeing Olin, she understood why she could not see a face in her dream. He too must have been monochromatic like this one standing in front of her, face to face. Having some strength to speak, she agreed with her elder saying,

"Yes, it would be an honor to our tribe for you to rest with us for a while."

"No, the honor would be mine." Turning to Inol he asked,

"Which way do we go?" Inol stepped through the edge of the tall grass. Without hesitation, Olin picked Ilon up in his forearms. Holding her close to him, Olin whispered to her,

"Do you know you smell like honey?" Laying her across his back, he followed the elder. Then the tall grass, wispy and thin, closed behind them like a curtain.

Honey Is Where The Heart Is

The Names Thereof

And out of the ground the Lord God formed every beast of the field and every fowl of the air; and brought them unto Adam to see what he would call them; and whatsoever Adam called every living creature, that was the name thereof…Genesis 2:19 KJV

1. Admiral: Larinda
2. Ant: Tan
3. Bee: Eeb
4. Beetle: Letebe
5. Bird: Drib
6. Butterfly: Flutterby
7. Caterpillar: Tarcaprille
8. Dove: Edvo
9. Finch: Ch'fin
10. Fly: Lyf
11. Honey
    a. Enhoy
    b. Hyeon
    c. Nyohe
    d. Onehy
    e. Onyhe
    f. Y'nohe
12. Hornet: Noreth
13. Hummingbird: Ghimmundrib
14. Lion: Onli
    a. Ilon (daughter)
    b. Inol (father)
    c. Lino (mother)
    d. Noli (youngster)
    e. Olin (stranger)
15. Monarch: Romchan
    a. Charmon
    b. Narchom
16. Oriole: Leorio
17. Panther
    a. Anpreth

    b. Napreth
18. Skipper: Kippers
19. Sunbird: Nusdrib
20. Swallowtail: Waltsaillow
21. Viceroy: Yorcive
22. Wasp: Spaw
23. Zebra: Breza

Made in the USA
Middletown, DE
20 June 2021